M000072653

The Ghost Files

Volume 3.5

By Apryl Baker

The Ghost Files - V3.5

Copyright © 2015 by Apryl Baker.
All rights reserved.
First Print Edition: December 2015

Limitless Publishing, LLC
Kailua, HI 96734
www.limitlesspublishing.com

Formatting: Limitless Publishing

ISBN-13: 978-1-68058-383-0
ISBN-10: 1-68058-383-2

No part of this book may be reproduced, scanned, or distributed in any printed or electronic form without permission. Please do not participate in or encourage piracy of copyrighted materials in violation of the author's rights. Thank you for respecting the hard work of this author.

This is a work of fiction. Names, characters, places, and incidents either are the product of the author's imagination or are used fictitiously, and any resemblance to locales, events, business establishments, or actual persons—living or dead—is entirely coincidental.

Dedication

For all the Ghost Files fans.
You are the reason this series exists.
I love you all! ☺

Chapter One

Caleb Malone cut the engine on his Ford pickup and stared at the Charlotte Police Department building, dread heavy in his heart. A hand ran through the wavy locks of his chocolaty brown hair, and he took a deep, steadying breath. His brother Eli stared at the building, but for an entirely different reason. Well, maybe not entirely. It started and ended with Mattie Louise Hathaway, Ghost Girl extraordinaire.

They'd met Mattie when Dr. Olivet, the leading parapsychologist in the country, asked her to join them on a ghost hunt in an old plantation home in New Orleans. He'd explained that her gift differed from that of the Malones'. Caleb's family could see and destroy ghosts that had turned evil, ones that didn't cross over for whatever reason and ended up filled with hate. Mattie, on the other hand, could see *all* ghosts, the good and bad ones.

For Caleb, she'd brought his world crashing down when she pulled Dan Richards into their life. Dan turned out to be his brother, a brother he didn't

1

know he had.

Dan had come to New Orleans to tell Mattie what he'd found out about the investigation he'd launched into her mother's background in hopes of finding her father.

What Dan had found was a connection to his own adoptive mother instead. She turned out to be Mattie's mom's sister. It had been very confusing at first. Caleb and Eli had eavesdropped on their conversation. What he heard shocked him. Dan's mother had apparently stolen him. Not just stolen him, but murdered his biological mother to do it.

His biological mother?

Amelia Malone, Caleb's mother.

That information was what had him sitting here right now, unease curling in the pit of his stomach.

Ann Richards had been arrested, and they were all here for questioning. He didn't know what to expect, how he'd respond if he saw the woman who had murdered his mother and stolen his brother. Would he stay calm or explode in rage? He felt it growing inside him. Had felt it kindle to life when he'd heard Dan tell Mattie about what his mother had done, not just to him, but to them all.

"Ready?" Eli asked, and Caleb glanced over at him. He looked apprehensive, jittery. Caleb almost felt sorry for him. Considering who Mattie was to Eli, he *should* feel sorry for his little brother, but he couldn't bring himself to. Despite the chaos she'd brought to their lives, she was a very special young girl who needed Eli, and Eli needed her. His brother needed someone to put him in his place. Mattie certainly did that.

"Are *you*?" he countered and laughed at the grimace Eli gave him.

"Dude, she's in there, and I just, I don't know…what am I supposed to say to her?"

"Hello?" Caleb said sarcastically.

Eli shot him an irritated glare and then got out of the truck. He shoved his hands in his pockets and waited. Caleb let out a long sigh and joined him after locking the truck. They both stared at the building for a moment and then went in together. Their father, James Malone, should already be there. After checking in with the desk sergeant, they sat down and waited.

Detective Grady came out to greet them, explaining that he wasn't sure if the detective in charge of the case would want to interview them or not. Their father had thought it best they both be there, just in case.

Caleb couldn't fathom why they'd be needed. Neither of them knew anything. If it had been left up to him, he'd have stayed home and helped his mother unpack in the cookie-cutter house they'd just bought. It was a new build, so aside from some cleaning, they had nothing to do but move in.

He smiled thinking of his mom's face when she'd seen the house. They'd lived in one rental unit after another for years. Other than a few knickknacks, they didn't really own any actual furniture, not even beds. His dad had always rented furnished homes or apartments. They needed to be able to move at the drop of a hat with his father's job in the FBI.

Heather Malone had been nagging his dad for

months about settling down in a home base for their little brother Ben's sake. He needed a stable home, a good school. Moving all the time was screwing up his education. The kid had issues reading, and even Caleb knew Ben needed a school where he could spend more than a few weeks or months in order to get a proper educational foundation.

He spotted his dad talking to someone, but his attention was focused on Eli. The boy had zeroed in on Mattie Hathaway. She was slumped against a wall looking miserable. Eli nodded to his dad and then wandered over to her. Caleb turned to his dad, but before he could say anything, a whirlwind of blond hair caught his eye.

She was talking to a woman who had to be her mother, as similar as they looked. Her face was animated with a myriad of emotions as she argued. All that blond hair was swishing back and forth with each angry hand movement. He smiled, thinking she looked cute, all irate and flustered. It wasn't until they started walking toward him that he noticed her limp. It wasn't a small one; it was very pronounced. What had happened to cause it?

"Caleb."

He turned to see his dad waving him over. He shot one more glance at the girl and then walked over to his father. "Eli seems to have irritated Mattie already."

They both turned to see her glaring daggers at Eli. "Well, they're stuck with each other for a while," James Malone said. "How are you holding up, son? I know this has to be hard on you."

Caleb shrugged. "I'm fine, Dad. Don't worry

about me."

Caleb was saved from further scrutiny when the detective in charge of his mother's case came out and called his dad back for questioning. She looked tough, but very businesslike.

Since everyone was busy, he slipped out of the room and walked outside. As much as he wanted to be there, he just couldn't. He wasn't ready to face all of it yet. So instead of listening to everyone talk about the situation, he sat down on the steps and looked over at the park across the street.

Kids were playing, moms and nannies sitting, occasionally calling out to a child. It was so normal. He hadn't known normal since…well, ever. He'd been raised in the ghost hunting business. That was *his* normal, and it sucked. His dad would be disappointed if he ever heard Caleb say that, so he kept it to himself, but he wanted normal more than anything in the world.

He'd gotten his degree online, and now his dad was pressuring him to join the Bureau. It wasn't what he wanted. He wanted to go to medical school, to become a surgeon, to help people. People who were alive, not the souls of people who had turned bitter and angry. To be able to fix someone, to give them back their chance to live again, that was what he wanted, but his dad? His dad believed it was foolish. James Malone thought Caleb, as the first-born, should carry out his responsibility in the family business.

He stared at nothing, his mind whirling with thoughts, regrets, and lost opportunities. How had he managed to get here? When had he gotten so lost in everyone else's dreams, he'd forfeited his own? His bitter laugh echoed around him as he thought about how he was always the good son, the one who never disobeyed and always did what was best for everyone besides himself. It got old sometimes. Caleb wished he could be selfish, wished he could do what was right for *him* instead of his family, but he wasn't selfish.

He sighed and stood, but before he could go back inside, a little boy caught his attention. He was about two, maybe three years old. He sat by himself in the sandbox, happily playing. Nothing should have made Caleb look at him twice, but something did. He walked over to the park and as close to the sandbox as he dared. He didn't want anyone yelling about a strange man perving the children. The little boy laughed, the melodic sound happy and content. His dark curls waved with each pass of the wind through the trees. What about this kid made Caleb stare at him?

"Caleb?"

He turned his head when he heard his name. It was the blonde from the police station. How did she know his name?

"I'm Mary Cross," she said, a smile tilting her lips. "Mattie is staying with me."

"You're a foster kid?" He couldn't help but notice the beautiful blue shade of her eyes or the laughter that brimmed in them.

She laughed. "No. Mattie is staying with me and my mom. We kinda took her in after what happened."

"You mean with her last foster home?" he asked,

remembering the girl's last foster mother turned out to be a serial killer who'd held her captive and tortured her for days before she escaped.

"Yeah." Some of the light went out of her eyes at the memory. "My mom and I wanted to give her a real home after she saved me. She deserves to be somewhere people understand who she is, what she can do. Where she won't be judged."

"She saved you?"

Mary nodded. Caleb could see her almost shrink in on herself, her posture hunching slightly. She shivered and wrapped her arms around herself. "I was Mrs. Olsen's last victim. I'd be dead if Mattie and Dan hadn't found me."

"Is that how you got your limp?" Caleb mentally slapped himself. How stupid could he be? He usually had better control over his mouth than this. It wasn't polite to ask someone that, especially a victim of violence.

"Um..."

"I'm sorry," he said. "That was rude. It's none of my business, really."

"No, it's okay," she murmured. "Yes, my limp was caused by what she did to me. I don't like to talk about it, though." Her gaze swept the park. "So, what are you doing out here? I thought you'd be inside with your family."

"I just needed some air." His attention swung back to the little boy and his shadows. He frowned and looked closer. Two shadows danced on the ground where there should be only one.

"Do you hear that?" Mary asked, her head cocked.

"What?" Caleb only heard the normal sounds of the playground, the kids, and the adults talking.

She stepped closer to the sandbox. "I don't know. It sounds like whispering?"

"We're in a playground full of kids. There's lots of whispering going on."

"I guess," she said, her voice thoughtful.

She had a nice voice too, soft and feminine. Caleb frowned and took a step back. She was still in high school, and he was too old for her. "Do you and Mattie go to school together?" he asked, the devil in him refusing to stay silent.

"No," she said. "I'm going to UNC in the fall. Mattie's still in high school."

"You're in college?"

"Yeah, it'll be my first year." A smile lit her face just a little. "How about you? Where do you go to school?"

"I graduated already." He stuffed his hands in his pockets, much like his brother had done earlier. It was a habit of theirs when they were nervous, and he could admit to himself this bundle of sunshine made him excessively nervous.

"Oh," she said. "So where do you work?"

"Nowhere yet." He scuffed his shoe against the ground. "I only just graduated."

"What did you major in?"

"Biology," he told her, "with an associate in psych."

"Awesome." She grinned up at him. "So, Mattie says you and your family are kinda like her? You see ghosts?"

Caleb stared, his own brown eyes widening. Did

8

she really just ask him that?

"What?" she asked, her voice all innocent. "I'm not supposed to know that or something? My mom and I know all about Mattie's gifts. It's how she saved me."

"What?" he asked, still reeling from her original question.

She laughed at his expression. "Let's just say I had an experience of my own that makes me believe her. She's not crazy, and neither are you."

Caleb took a deep breath and then another one. She talked about their abilities like she was asking him if he played basketball or something.

"I'm not crazy either." She gave him a rueful look. "It's okay if you don't want to talk about it, though."

"Mary?"

They turned to see a woman in her mid-thirties or so coming over to stand by them. "I thought I recognized you."

"Mrs. Flynn," Mary greeted her. "It's good to see you again. This is Caleb Malone. The Flynns are our next-door neighbors. Mom says congratulations are in order."

Mrs. Flynn scooped up the little boy they'd both been watching. "Yes, this is Noah. We just got him last week."

"Hi, Noah," Mary cooed at the baby. "Mom said she'd met him, but she never said he was such a cutie."

"He is, isn't he?" Mrs. Flynn said proudly. "We've been on the adoption list for two years. We couldn't believe it when we got the call. Anthony and I wanted to talk to you about maybe babysitting for us."

"Sure. Why don't you guys come over to the house tomorrow and we'll talk about it? I really need to get back inside. Mom's probably ready to leave by now."

"Of course." Mrs. Flynn nodded. "We'll see you tomorrow. I'm looking forward to meeting Mattie."

Caleb stared after them as they walked away, troubled. Something was wrong there. He could see a double shadow on the ground. At least he knew where they lived, and he could check it out. If he could see and sense something, there might be a malignant force attached to the baby. Never a good thing. Definitely worth looking into.

"I'm gonna head back inside," Mary said. "You coming?"

"Yeah." He nodded and followed her across the road and back into the CPD building. His dad motioned him over as soon as he saw them. Mary made a beeline for her mother.

"Where did you go?" His father gave him a questioning look.

"Just needed some air." Caleb's eyes strayed to where Mary was talking to her mom.

"Uh-huh," his dad said, the laugh in his voice making Caleb cringe a little.

"Where's everyone?" Eli, Mattie, and Dan were missing.

"Dan took Mattie home, and Eli tagged along. It's been a rough day for her."

"Yeah, I can imagine."

"Seriously, Mom?" Mary's voice carried across

the room. "Mattie doesn't even have a key to get inside. We have to go let her in before you go to the AT&T store to fix your phone."

"Mary, I need my phone for work. It won't take us long. I'm sure Mattie will be fine waiting for a few minutes. Dan's with her."

"I can take Mary home," Caleb volunteered. The words were out of his mouth before he could stop them. Another mental slap. What was wrong with him today? He should have stayed out of it, but he liked her. There, he admitted it. He liked the ball of sunshine that was Mary Cross.

"I don't know..." Mrs. Cross frowned.

"Mom, Caleb is Dan's brother and the son of an *FBI* agent." The exasperation was clear in Mary's voice. "I'll be perfectly safe with him."

"You call me as soon as you get home."

Mary rolled her eyes, but grabbed her purse from her mom and walked over to Caleb. "Let's go before she changes her mind."

Caleb glanced down into her smiling face and almost groaned. She might be perfectly safe with him, but would he be safe with her?

Chapter Two

Caleb glanced over at Mary. She was humming along to some boy band on the radio. She had a beautiful singing voice too. It was soft and whimsical. She'd turned the radio station to KISS 95.1 as soon as she'd climbed in the truck. He had to admit, they played pretty good tunes. He'd been worried she'd be into some pop channel, but this one had a good balance of everything.

"Talking about your gift really freaks you out, doesn't it?" Mary asked, startling Caleb out of his thoughts.

"No."

"Uh-huh. It freaks Mattie too, so you're not alone. I don't think either of you should feel that way, though. What you guys can do is super awesome. Being able to help people like that? It's cool."

"My gift isn't like Mattie's. I don't help ghosts." He still couldn't get over how casual she sounded about his peculiar abilities.

"Then what do you do?" she asked, curious. "I

mean, you don't have to tell me if you don't want to."

Caleb bit back a smile at her pouty expression. He had a feeling this girl always got what she wanted. If she already knew about his gifts, what was the harm in explaining things to her?

"My family can see ghosts, but only after they've gone vengeful. When a ghost is on this plane for too long, they begin to get angry and more confused. That anger turns to rage, and all they want is to hurt the living the way they are hurting. Their anger gives them the energy to cause the living physical harm. Once they reach the nuclear meltdown stage, they become visible to us. We hunt them down and take care of the problem."

Mary looked thoughtful while she pondered that, and Caleb glanced at her several times out of the corner of his eye. What she finally said was not what he expected. "You end their suffering and send them to where they're supposed to be. So, yes, your gift *is* just as super awesome as Mattie's."

Caleb laughed; he couldn't help himself. No one had ever seen the good in his gift or gotten all excited about it before. Mary was definitely a unique girl. And sweet.

"Take this exit and turn right." She pointed to the sign up ahead. "It's a pain if you miss it."

"I've noticed the city has a strange layout." Caleb slowed down and took the exit. "We got turned around a couple times when we missed our turnoff."

"Yup, that's the Queen City for you." Mary grinned. "Miss your exit and you have to jump through hoops to turn around and get back to where you need to be. So aside from learning the roads, how do you like it down here? Different from where you were before?"

"Well, we travel a lot," he told her. "Dad's never really settled in one place for too long because of his work, and he always packed us up and moved us with him."

"That had to suck growing up." Mary fiddled with the air, turning it up just a little higher. "I'd hate having to try and make new friends all the time. It's tough enough holding on to the ones you've known for years, let alone finding new ones."

Caleb glanced over to see her staring out the window. The hurt in her voice spoke volumes about what she'd been through. Her limp might have caused some of her friends to not be so friendly anymore. High school kids were vicious when it came to things like that. He felt a surge of anger rise within him at the thought of anyone causing this girl pain, and he frowned. No one had ever sparked a reaction in him so quickly.

"After the first few times, you learn not to make attachments with anyone," he said finally. "It's easier that way." Caleb would do well to remember that now. He'd known this girl for less than an hour, and he was already feeling attached.

"Yeah, I get that, but not making any kind of attachment? That has to suck just as much. Everyone needs someone, Caleb, even if only for a few weeks."

The simple truth of that statement struck Caleb

The Ghost Files - V3.5

as probably one of the wisest things he'd ever heard. His mother would love this girl.

"Well, for better or worse, Charlotte is our home now. Dad wants us to get to know Dan, and putting down roots will be good for our little brother Ben, at least. He needs some stability."

"And you never know," Mary said. "You might actually find a friend or two."

"Maybe," Caleb agreed, a smile tugging at his lips at her sly tone.

"Right here." Mary pointed to the left. "This is our street. Third house on the left."

They saw Mattie, Eli, and Dan sitting on the front porch. Mary had been right about them sitting and waiting. Before Caleb managed to put the truck in park, Mary jumped out and bounced up the steps. He laughed at her and almost ran to catch up to her.

"Need this?" Caleb watched the grin fade from Mary's face, and she asked, "What's wrong?"

"What isn't wrong?" Mattie laughed bitterly.

"The fact that you're curled up in a hottie's lap?" Mary smirked.

"Yeah, there is that." Mattie smiled. "Eli, this is Mary Cross, my foster sister."

"Just sister," Mary corrected her, her face stern. "Skip the foster bit. I told you. You're my sister, and that's that."

"I have a feeling Mary gets whatever she wants," Caleb said, remembering thinking just that earlier. This girl truly was a force of nature. He shook his head and followed them all inside, hearing Mary say she'd go with Mattie upstairs to get some drawings.

"Drawings?" he asked as soon as they'd settled themselves in the living room.

"Mattie can draw," Eli explained. "She's being haunted by some dead girls blaming her for their murder. She's gonna draw us pictures of what they look like."

"She any good?"

"Better than good," Dan said, a smile dancing on his face. "You'll understand once you see them. Just be prepared."

"Prepared?" he and Eli asked together.

"Mattie draws them the way she sees them when they first come to her, and considering they're dead…well, it can be pretty gruesome."

A few minutes later, both girls were back. Mary went to fix them lunch, and Mattie settled down to draw. Half an hour later, she pronounced she was done and handed the sketches to Dan. Curious, Caleb peeked over Dan's shoulder at the images. He gasped. The drawings were brutal, detailed, and haunting. They were also very disturbing. He glanced over at Mattie, who watched them with a worried expression. If he had to guess, showing her work to people wasn't something she did a lot.

"Wow, Mattie, these are…" He trailed off, not knowing what word to use.

"Gruesome?" Eli asked, clearly fascinated.

"Beautiful," Dan corrected. "Dark, moody, and gruesome, but beautiful."

Mattie beamed at him, and Caleb shook his head. Dan might not understand his own feelings for Mattie, but the two of them shared a bond he didn't think Eli would ever touch. There was a certain light around them that connected them.

Caleb's gift was unique in and of itself. He could see auras sometimes, but only if the person's emotions were so strong it would register as a ten on the Richter scale, or when people's connections to each other defied time and space. That was the kind of bond she shared with both of his brothers. The bonds they shared were different, but sometime down the road, she was going to have to choose between the two. Caleb dreaded it because all three of them would end up hurt.

"Can you get a hit off the facial recognition software with these?" Mattie asked, pulling Caleb back into the conversation.

"Ohhh, do we have a case?" Mary chirped, coming out of the kitchen carrying a plate of subs. Caleb tried to help her, but she shooed him away, making him frown. The girl needed to learn to accept a little help.

"No, *we* don't have a case," Dan told her. "*I* have a case."

Caleb felt a low growl building. He did not like Dan talking to her in that snotty manner, but before he could say anything, Eli did. "No, actually, I believe *Mattie* has a case. You have jack without her."

"Will both of you stop it?" Mattie demanded. "If Mary wants to help, then she can. You have enough to worry about right now anyway, *Officer Dan*. How do you expect to have time to trudge around looking for clues? Your dad and Cam need you more than I do right now."

Dan's face paled. Caleb had forgotten about

what was going on. Mary had managed to distract him enough to let him breathe for a few minutes.

"Because you have Eli?" Dan snarled, and Caleb's earlier thoughts came rushing back. Dan had no idea how much he loved Mattie, how much he was in love with her. When he finally figured it out, it was going to be bad for them all. Eli and Mattie had a connection that couldn't be broken, no matter who she chose. Dan might end up getting hurt more than anyone.

They were all just trying to adjust to the fact they were brothers, and this thing with Mattie might destroy whatever chance they had of being a family. He wanted to blame Mattie, but he couldn't. The same bond that connected her to Eli held a little sway over him as well because of their bloodline. His only thought was to protect the girl, but who was going to protect them from all the damage she was going to do their lives?

"That's it!" Mattie exploded. "Outside right now!"

Eli snickered as he watched the two of them march out the front door.

"Here, you two might as well eat while they work that out," Mary said. "I'll go grab you guys a drink. I have water, Mountain Dew, and Coke."

"Mountain Dew," Caleb told her, and Eli agreed. She was only gone a minute, and then returned and handed them each a cold can of soda.

"Got a question for you, bro," Eli said. "Mattie has a problem. Seems that when a ghost touches her, they can make her feel everything they felt when they died. One of the ghosts who thinks she's responsible for their death attacked her at the airport earlier. Is there a way to protect her from that? A sigil or rune, maybe?"

Caleb stared out the window thoughtfully. There might be. It was a really old rune, but with some changes, it might do what she needed. He couldn't imagine what he'd feel like if he were forced to relive a ghost's death every time one of them touched him. It had to be unnerving, and maybe painful too.

Eli grabbed two of the sandwiches and started scarfing like he hadn't eaten in days. It was disgusting to watch. Even Mary stared at him, fascinated at the way he shoveled the sandwiches into his mouth. When Mattie and Dan returned, Eli looked up and gave them both a grin full of food.

"Mouth closed," Caleb told his brother. "You'd think Mom never taught you any manners."

Eli just shrugged. Dan loaded his own plate, took a seat beside Eli, and started to inhale his food. Caleb could only stare at the two of them. They were both eating like they were in a contest. Well, there was one trait they had in common—they were both gluttons.

"Mattie, Eli told me about what happened earlier. There's an old rune I think will work, but I need to study it and make sure the changes I make to it are right."

"How can you tell if you get it right?" she asked, her tone curious.

"We won't know till we try it," Caleb said. "Eli will ink you when I finally settle on the design. He's better at that than I am."

"Is there anything I can do to keep the ghosts out of the house?"

For a girl with ghost abilities, she sure didn't know much about them. "You can salt all the doors and windows. If someone breaks the salt line, though, it becomes useless."

"Salt?" Surprise colored Mary's question. "Why salt?"

"Salt is a natural absorbent," Caleb explained, grabbing the last sandwich before either of his brothers could. He hadn't eaten all day, and he was starving. No point in letting their disgusting habits ruin his appetite. "It basically absorbs the energy a ghost gives off and acts as a natural barrier because of it."

Dan's phone rang, and he took it and his plate of sandwiches outside. From the look on his face, it had to be about his mom. Caleb felt conflicted. He wanted to say something to help Dan, but at the same time, he couldn't. Dan's adoptive mother killed their birth mother. Caleb just couldn't console him when it came to Ann Richards.

He looked up to find Mary staring at him. She gave him a reassuring smile, and he had the oddest feeling she knew exactly what he'd been thinking. Maybe she did. The girl was very perceptive.

"Does he always eat like that?" Mary pointed to Eli.

"Unfortunately, yes. I've seen him take down some of the best hot dog eating champions in the world."

"Hey, I'm a growing boy," Eli said when he swallowed the rest of his last sub. "You going to eat that?"

"Touch it and die," Caleb told his brother, ice in his voice.

Eli shrugged and turned his attention to Mattie. "Did you eat, Hilda?"

Did his brother really ask Mattie if she'd eaten? Eli had never in his entire life inquired to see if anyone else was hungry, and that included his own family. Mattie made him remember someone's needs other than his own? Wow…just wow.

"Do you want me to make you one?" Eli's question made Caleb's eyes widen. He offered to make her food? Had the boy lost his mind? This was not his brother.

She cringed. "No, just watching you eat made me lose my appetite."

"You'll get used to it." A grin spread across Eli's face.

"No, I won't," she countered. "That implies you and I will be spending time together. Not gonna happen."

"Oh, Hilda, it's so gonna happen." Eli's grin got bigger. "I guarantee it."

"I would have to like you to spend time with you," she said. "Since I don't like you…I don't see that happening."

"You seriously wound me, Hilda." He faked a shot to his heart.

"He's adorable." Mary giggled.

"He's a pain," Mattie said, and Caleb agreed. "And don't call me Hilda!"

Caleb could see how angry Mattie was getting, and he'd bet anything she was about to give his brother another beat down even if Eli didn't see it coming. He insisted on calling her Hilda, something he'd devised from her name, Mathilda. She despised it. "Elijah," he warned. "Lay off unless you want to get thrashed. Again."

"Why not, Hilda? It's your name, isn't it?"

Mattie turned, and her fist landed in Eli's gut before he or Caleb saw it coming. Eli bent over and Mattie grabbed his head and pulled it down to meet her knee as it came up. Eli coughed and toppled off the couch onto the floor. Mattie stood up and glared down at him. "Don't. Call. Me. Hilda! Got it?"

The screen door opened, and Dan stared at the scene in front of him a second before coming to stand behind Mattie. He laughed, and before Caleb knew it, he was laughing just as hard as Dan was.

Mary, however, wasn't laughing. "Mattie, you can't just hit people because…well, because…just because!"

Caleb shook his head and felt his phone vibrate. Ignoring them for a second, he pulled it out. It was from his dad. His parents were taking Ben to a movie, so he, Eli, and their sister, Ava, would have to fend for themselves tonight. Caleb caught movement out of the corner of his eye and saw Dan grab Mattie before she could do more damage to their brother.

"You seriously like to get beat up by girls, don't you?" Dan asked.

"Nah, I just like to irritate this one." Eli pushed himself up off the floor. "I need to watch out for that left hook of hers, though."

"On that note," Caleb said, "I better get him out

of here before Mattie really does hurt him. It was nice to meet you, Mary."

"You too." Mary grinned at him, and he couldn't help but smile back.

"Mattie, I'll call you when I get that tattoo worked out, okay?"

"Thanks, Caleb." Mattie gave him a hug, and he ruffled her hair. He had this insane need to protect her, kinda like he had with Ava, almost like a sister.

Caleb took his brother by the arm and hauled him toward the door. "Let's go, Elijah."

Once they were in the truck, he shook his head. "You do like getting beat up by girls, don't you?"

"I let her do it," Eli defended, a blush ghosting over his cheeks.

"Bull." Caleb laughed. "You finally met a girl who's too much for even you to handle."

"And what about you?" Eli asked. "Don't think I didn't see the way you were watching Mary."

"She's nice," Caleb said. "I was only being nice in return."

"Yeah, right, bro. You stalked her with your eyes the entire time we were there."

Caleb glanced out his window and saw the woman and little boy from the park. She was chatting with a neighbor by the fence, and the child was playing in the yard with some blocks. Caleb squinted, and sure enough, there were still two shadows attached to the kid.

"Eli, look over there at the baby playing. What do you see?"

Eli turned his head and studied the kid for a minute, then his eyes narrowed. "Why does he have two shadows?"

"That's what I want to know," Caleb said. "They were at the park across from the police station earlier. I saw it then."

"Why were they at that park? That's a good half hour drive from here."

"No clue," Caleb said. "We should look into it, though. Whatever has attached itself to the kid isn't good at all."

"No," Eli agreed. "At least we might be able to get close this time without looking like some weird pedophiles scoping out children."

Caleb laughed. Eli had been called just that once by a mother who had been targeted by an angry spirit. She'd apologized later, of course, but it had rankled Eli since the incident.

"Any ideas what it might be?" Eli's face was thoughtful. "I can't think of anything offhand."

"No idea. We need to check with Dad to see if he's run into something like this before. First, though, we need to pick up dinner. Mom and Dad took Ben to the movies."

"Pizza," Eli said without hesitation, and Caleb agreed. They'd all eat pizza, even Ava, who was on a vegetarian kick this week. He pulled out of the drive and glanced back one more time at the little boy with two shadows, his thoughts troubled. Something was very wrong there.

He didn't know what, but he would.

Chapter Three

Mary watched Caleb work, a dreamy smile plastered on her face. He was simply gorgeous. All that dark brown hair and those chocolate eyes...*mmm*. He was nice too. The fact that he was back made her day. Mattie had come home from the hospital to discover the ghost-proofing actually banned her from the house. Caleb had to take it all down.

Mattie needed the house demon-proofed as well. The demon who had been stalking her showed up in her bedroom. Despite the fact Mary claimed she was cool with all the supernatural stuff surrounding her new foster sister, the thought of a demon in her home majorly freaked her out. Mary was glad Caleb knew how to keep them out.

He'd explained to her earlier demons weren't all like what she saw on TV. Sure, some of them were just as evil as those portrayed in movies. They took over a person's body to consume their souls, some made deals with humans—who sold their souls for what they wanted most. Demons were like humans.

Some were smart, some were clever, some simply followed orders, and some were slightly less evil than the others. Caleb admitted they'd worked with a few demons in the past when it was necessary.

No matter what kind of demon had attached itself to Mattie, Mary wanted it out of her house without the ability to return. Ghosts too. Mattie's latest hospital visit resulted from an angry ghost who'd tried to kill her. Well, the ghost had technically succeeded in drowning her.

If it hadn't been for Eli and Caleb, she'd have been good and dead. Mary didn't know CPR, something she was rectifying this weekend, especially with Mattie living here. Having a sister with supernatural abilities meant adjusting more than Mary had originally thought, but she wouldn't change a thing. Mattie had saved her life, and giving her a home was the least she could do.

A knock sounded at the door, and Mary frowned. She'd have to give up her perch watching Caleb's behind as he worked. Sigh. She pulled herself up and went to open the door. Mrs. Flynn and her new baby stood on the porch. She looked tired.

"Hello, Mary, can we come in?"

"Of course." Mary stood back to let them enter, hoping against hope Caleb would hear they had company and cover up the symbols he was engraving in the walls. She led them past the living room and into the kitchen. They didn't have an open concept home. Instead, the kitchen was in a room by itself. "Can I get you some tea, Mrs. Flynn?"

"Yes, thank you." She put the baby down on the floor and settled a few toys around him before taking a seat at the kitchen table. "I've been so busy with Noah, I haven't had time to sit for even a moment."

Mary poured her a glass of iced tea and took a seat across from her. She looked more than tired, she looked drained. "Noah not adjusting well?"

Mrs. Flynn gave her a rueful look. "Is it that obvious?"

"You look a little tired. I figured he hasn't been sleeping through the night. You've only had him a little over a week or so?"

Mrs. Flynn nervously tapped her fingernails on the table. "Yes, that's right. Normally, he's such a good baby, but at night when we put him down...well, he doesn't stay down for long."

"He'll get used to it soon enough," Mary assured her. "Babies adapt quickly."

"I hope so," she said, her voice a little pained. "I came to see if you still wanted to babysit for us."

"Yeah." Mary leaned over and ruffled the baby's soft hair. He looked up and grinned at her. "He and I will get along just fine."

Mrs. Flynn looked relieved. "Anthony and I have tried two different babysitters this week. We didn't want to bother you with everything going on with Mattie."

"No worries," Mary told the woman. "It's all good. I'll be happy to babysit for y'all."

"How about tomorrow night?" Mrs. Flynn asked. "We need to be at the mayor's for a dinner party. Anthony was just promoted to Deputy Chief."

"Oh, wow. Tell him congratulations for me. What time do you need me to be there?"

"Is six okay?"

"Sure is. I normally charge twenty an hour, but for you guys, I'll do it for ten."

"Thank you, sweetie," she said.

"You said you'd tried two different babysitters?" Mary asked, thinking it sounded odd.

"Noah hasn't liked either of them," Mrs. Flynn admitted. "He cried the entire time we were gone, and..."

"And?" Mary prompted when she stopped.

Mrs. Flynn let out a long sigh. "Well, they both said strange things happened while we were gone."

"Strange things?" Mary felt a frown settle on her face.

"It's nothing," Mrs. Flynn assured her. "I think the baby's constant crying got the best of them." She stood up and collected Noah. "I'll see you tomorrow, Mary. Please tell your mother to not be such a stranger."

Mary walked them out, her mind reeling with questions. Something had disturbed Mrs. Flynn, and she didn't want to talk about it. What strange things had been happening? Was it only the babysitters who experienced it, or had the Flynns seen the strange things firsthand? Had it started when Noah came to live with them, or had it been happening for a while?

Come tomorrow night, she'd find out one way or another if something was going on in the house.

"What's wrong?"

Mary blinked at the sound of Eli Malone's voice. He was gazing up at her from the bottom step of the porch, his aqua eyes alert.

"Nothing," she said. "Come on inside. Caleb should be finishing up. Mattie's still asleep, so please don't wake her."

"Is she okay?"

Mary nodded. "Yeah. There was another ghost attack last night, but we took care of it."

"We have to figure out who these crazy ghost girls are soon. Any more attacks and she might not survive it."

Eli followed her inside and upstairs to where Caleb was working in the hallway. Mattie's door stood partially open, and Mary glanced in to make sure she was still asleep. A noise caught her attention and she paused. She listened, and sure enough, there it was again. She pushed the door open and slowly made her way inside, looking around.

Mattie was still sound asleep, and her TV off.

"Everything okay?" Eli poked his head in and looked around too.

"Yeah," Mary said and walked back out. It was quiet in there now.

"Mary, Eli said there was another ghost attack last night?"

She turned to see Caleb off the ladder and leaning against the wall. His muscles bulged, and it was all she could do to rip her eyes away from his tight t-shirt.

"Yes, but like I told Eli, we took care of it."

"We?" Caleb's expression was a mixture of censure and incredulity. "Mary, you don't need to be messing with things you don't understand. Mattie is equipped to deal with ghosts, *you're* not."

"Excuse me?"

"We're ghost hunters, Mary, and we know what we're doing. Mattie can take care of herself too, but you can't. You're just an ordinary girl with no idea what's really going on. You can get hurt, so stay out of it and let those of us who do know what we're doing handle things."

Did he seriously just order her to stay out of all things ghostly in that highhanded manner she'd ignored yesterday because she thought he was cute? *He did not!*

"So let me get this straight, Mr. Big Bad Ghost Hunter," she said, her voice soft. "I'm just a poor, helpless girl who has no clue about ghosts, and I need to mind my own business?"

"Basically, yes."

Eli let out a hiss and stepped back. Smart boy.

"Are you really as arrogantly stupid as you sound?" She could feel the expression on her face morph to one of rage. *How dare he?*

His eyes widened as she came closer. "Listen here, Caleb Malone. I *do* know about ghosts. I made sure I read everything I could get my hands on when we decided to have Mattie come stay here. Just because I'm some *girl* with no special superhero powers like you, doesn't mean I don't know the risks, or what I'm doing. How *dare* you presume to tell me what I can and can't do? I am not some stupid fangirl playing at ghost hunting. I'm intelligent, and I got myself up to speed on all things ghostly so I could help keep my sister safe."

Caleb's mouth worked for several seconds with no sound escaping before he managed to get control of it. She would have laughed if she weren't so pissed. Eli, however, had no issue laughing at his brother.

"I'm sorry," Caleb muttered. "I didn't mean to offend you. I was just…"

"Shh," Mary shushed him. She'd heard that noise from Mattie's room again. She went back in and stepped closer to the bed, listening. This time, the sounds were louder, more clear. There was a lot of hissing, moaning, and spooky sounds coming from the area around Mattie's bed.

"What is it?" Eli asked, coming to stand next to her, his head cocked.

"Do you hear that?"

"Hear what?" Caleb stood on her other side.

"You can't hear it?" The noises were loud.

"What?" Caleb asked again, his tone frustrated. "There's nothing here."

"I can hear things, weird sounds."

"What do you mean, you can hear things?" Caleb questioned.

"Around her bed," Mary informed him. "There are things whispering, moaning, and making generally unpleasant sounds."

"I don't hear anything, Mary." Caleb almost glared at her, and Mary shot him a look of irritation.

"Just because Mr. Big Bad Ghost Hunter can't hear it, that isn't *my* problem. The fact remains something is not right!" Mary's voice rose with each word.

"Good one, Mary." Eli laughed. "Give him what for."

"I already apologized," Caleb snapped. "Can't

you two just let it go?"

"Hey, I'm not the one who told her she needed to let the people who knew what they were doing handle things, and to let the big bad ghost hunter fix it."

"Well, it's true." Caleb sounded exasperated. "She's ordinary…she doesn't know how much she can get hurt…"

That was it. Mary's temper exploded. He had no right. None, especially after everything she'd been through.

"Really?" Mary asked, her voice going soft. "I'm *ordinary* and I don't know how much I can get hurt? I *survived* the torture of a crazy lady for *three weeks*. There are scars all over my body. I can't even walk without limping because she broke both my legs, my ankle, *and* snapped the tendons in my left foot. I've known more pain in my ordinary life than you *ever* will."

She turned and stomped out of the room, slamming the door to her own room when she got there. The door held her up as she fought to control her tears. He had no idea who she was, what she could and couldn't take.

Stupid man. A tear leaked out and rolled down her cheek. She wiped it away angrily. He thought she was *ordinary*? Of course he did. He hunted down ghosts. All his girlfriends were probably all big bad ghost hunters too. How was she supposed to compete with that?

And did she want to? She hated arrogant men, and he was probably one of the most arrogant she'd ever met. Not to mention he thought she was *ordinary.*

Her eyes narrowed. She'd show him ordinary.

***

Caleb all but growled in frustration. Mattie had informed them that Mary could indeed hear ghosts, and that he owed her a huge apology. How the heck was he supposed to know the girl could hear ghosts? He'd never even heard of anyone with that ability before.

Not only did he have Mary to deal with, but Eli needed a ride to the lake to chase after Mattie. She'd overheard their conversation about Eli being her guardian angel and ran, just like Eli had feared. How did he go from simple demon-proofing to being involved in teenage drama? Eli needed his own car.

"Are you two leaving?" Mary asked, her blue eyes still full of fire.

"We're going to the lake to find Mattie," Eli told her. "She ran out on me when I told her about the bond we share."

"Bond?"

"We don't have time to sit here and explain it if you want to catch your girlfriend," Caleb interrupted his brother. He just wanted this day to be over.

"Then you can explain it on the way to the lake," Mary decided, and she and Eli headed out the front door.

"Wait…" Caleb called, but they both ignored him and climbed into his truck. He closed his eyes and rubbed his forehead. He did not need this today.

He closed and locked the bottom lock on the door before dragging himself to the truck. When he climbed in, Eli was explaining the Guardian Angel bond to Mary, who was conveniently in the middle. He shifted, and his arm rubbed against hers. She smelled like peaches and warm honey. The scent invaded his nostrils and he inhaled deeply. It made him think things he shouldn't be thinking.

"Are you just gonna sit there all day, or are we going to the lake?" Mary snapped, bringing him out of his thoughts.

Instead of answering, he started the truck and backed out. He knew the lake was in Mooresville or Davidson, so he drove until he hit I-77 North. Mary wouldn't let him miss the right exit. At least he hoped not.

Eli's phone buzzed, and he answered it. "Hey, Ava." He listened for a minute. "No, we're going to the lake to catch up with Mattie and Dan…Sure, we can come get you."

Caleb groaned. These people needed their own transportation in a bad way. Instead of arguing, he took the next exit. He could get to their house from there.

"So you can really hear ghosts?" Eli asked.

"Yes." Mary's voice was back to the soft tone Caleb was used to. "It started after…"

"You were never able to before?"

She shook her head. "I remember every moment of what happened to me, even when I went to visit Mattie during the quiet times."

"Visit Mattie?" Eli frowned. "Wait, do you mean

an out-of-body experience?"

Mary shrugged. "I guess. I don't know what you'd call it. Mattie says I was close to death and my soul traveled to her. She came and found me. If it wasn't for her, I'd be dead."

"Dan told me about what happened to both of you," Eli said. "Can I ask you a question?"

"Sure."

"When you went to visit Mattie, could you hear the ghosts then?"

Mary was quiet for a moment, but then she nodded. "Yeah. That's how I found out about her. They told me about a girl who could see and hear them. When I thought about her, it's like this bright path appeared in front of me. I just followed it straight to her. She was lit up like a Christmas tree."

That made sense, Caleb thought. The Doc said Mattie was a beacon to ghosts, her energy lighting up so they could see her. Mary must have been so close to death, her soul could tap into the energy Mattie naturally exuded.

"So the ghosts never shut up after you woke up?" Eli questioned.

Again, Mary took a few minutes to think about her answer. "I never really thought of it that way. It was muted when I woke up, but it got stronger as the weeks went by. Now, if I focus, I can hear them." She shivered. "There are so many around us all the time. People have no idea they are never more than three steps away from a ghost."

"Seriously?" Eli asked.

"Yes." Mary smiled at him. "I forget you guys can't see them all, or hear them like I can. You only see the bad ones."

"You've officially creeped me out," Eli said. "I didn't need to know that."

Mary laughed. "I think you can handle it."

Caleb wasn't sure he could, though. Hearing ghosts wasn't normal, even in their line of work. Granted, he'd never met someone who had gone through what Mary had either.

Feeling like a first class jerk wasn't something he was used to. He'd behaved like an arrogant idiot, and he needed to apologize to her, but it wasn't something he looked forward to. Saying *I'm sorry* didn't happen often to Caleb. Maybe he could get her alone at the lake and talk to her.

A smile flirted with his lips when he thought of her blue eyes spitting fire at him. She was a firecracker. She had nerve too, inviting herself along. Most girls he knew wouldn't have done that, not even his sister, Ava.

Mary just kept surprising him, and he liked it more than he should.

Caleb pulled into his parents' driveway and honked the horn. Ava came running out, jumping into a pair of shorts as she ran. She looked so much like their mother, it always amazed Caleb. The two could be twins instead of mother and daughter. The only difference was Ava had brown eyes instead of Heather's aqua ones.

"Hi!" Ava climbed into the back seat of the cab. "I'm Ava."

"This is Mary, Mattie's foster sister," Caleb introduced as he backed back out and headed for the interstate. They were going to miss Mattie and Dan with all these side stops.

"Is traffic always this bad?" Eli complained a while later. They were sitting still on I-77, creeping every few minutes.

Mary chuckled, the sound almost musical, and it made Caleb want to smile. "It's summer. Lake Norman is a hot spot during the season. It'll get better once we hit the Huntersville exit and then slow down again the closer we get to the lake. People bottleneck traffic looking at the boats."

Eli snorted. "More like hoping to see some topless girls."

"That too." Amusement tinged her voice as she fiddled with the air conditioning.

What should have been a half-hour drive took them almost two hours, since they had to backtrack and retrieve their sister. She'd been dying to meet Mattie.

Eli, Ava, and Mary chatted mostly about Mattie. Caleb noticed whenever they asked about Mary herself, she always turned the topic to something else. It made him curious as to why she was so closed off.

When they finally reached the lake and found a parking spot, Caleb all but jumped out of the truck. Being so close to Mary for so long had been a little unnerving. The girl affected him in ways no one else had.

"She's that way," Eli announced.

"How do you know?" Mary asked.

"Guardian Angel bond."

Caleb grinned at Mary's dumbfounded look. That bond took some getting used to. Basically, Eli had an internal GPS when it came to Mattie's location. He'd always know where she was.

"They could be anywhere," Mary argued.

Eli shrugged. "I'm going east. Why don't you guys try that way?"

Mary sighed and turned to look at Caleb. Her expression turned grumpy. "Come on, Mr. Big Bad Ghost Hunter, let's go find them."

"Do I even want to ask?"

"No," they both said at the same time, and Ava burst out laughing, throwing her blonde hair over one shoulder.

"Do you two need a time out?"

"He does," Mary grumbled and started walking.

Caleb shot a glare at his sister and hurried to catch up. The ground was uneven, and he was worried Mary might stumble with her limp.

"Did he get all macho arrogant?" Ava asked, linking her arm with Mary's. Caleb figured she must have had the same thought he did about the terrain.

"Do that often, does he?"

"Oh, yeah." Ava nodded. "He tries that with me all the time. He thinks because I'm a girl I can't fight ghosts just as well as he can."

"Like that makes a difference?" Mary scoffed.

"Exactly," Ava agreed with a vigorous nod.

Caleb rolled his eyes.

"Speaking of ghost hunting, I think something is going on over at my neighbor's house," Mary said.

"Great, now she thinks she's the Nancy Drew of the ghost hunting world," Caleb muttered.

A gasp escaped both girls, and his eyes widened.

He didn't think he'd said that loud enough for them to hear, but they had. Two murderous faces were glaring at him.

"You did not go there," Mary seethed, looking like she wanted to send a fist his way.

Ava kicked him. "How dare you!"

"I'm sorry." Caleb threw up a hand to stop his sister from going off on him. "I'm tired, and I don't want to fight. Can we just please find Dan and Mattie?"

"Your brother may be cute, but he's an idiot," Mary told Ava.

She thought he was cute?

"Let's find Eli," Ava said. "I'm pretty sure he'll find Mattie before we do because of his bond with her."

"Whatever," Mary mumbled. She followed Ava in the direction Eli had gone.

Caleb let out a long sigh and then hurried to catch up with them. He'd hurt her feelings more than once today, and it was the last thing he'd wanted to do. He liked Mary, but he was mucking it up. What else could go wrong today?

Why did he ask those questions? He found himself on a boat with his brothers, Ava, Mattie, and Mary a short while later, looking for the place a girl was supposed to have gone missing. Not only that, but Mattie and Mary looked ready to hurl with each sway of the boat. It wasn't long before Dan found a secluded area with a dock to pull into. If it belonged to someone, they could always explain the girls were sick.

Caleb tried to help Mary, but she shoved his

hands away. "I'm fine."

"You're not fine," he growled, frustrated. He was trying to make up for his behavior earlier, but she was having none of it. "Let me help you down. You're sick, and the boat is wobbly. With your limp, I'm afraid you'll fall…"

Mary whirled on him, eyes blazing blue fire. "Just because I have a limp doesn't mean I'm an invalid. It doesn't make me any less of a person than someone who's perfect and unmarred!"

"I didn't mean…" His eyes widened as she came closer.

"You are a first class idiot who needs to learn to mind his manners. Didn't your mama teach you any? Cute you might be, but if you talk to all the girls like this, it's a wonder you ever had a girlfriend."

His nostrils flared as his own irritation rose. "Look here…"

"No, *you* look here," Mary interrupted him. "Go be a douche somewhere else!" She pushed him, and Caleb felt himself falling backward and let out a string of curse words when he hit the cold lake. He spit out water when he resurfaced and watched Mary stalk over to where Mattie was stretched out on the bank. She fell down beside her while he dragged himself out of the water.

Eli reached a hand to him and hauled him up. He grunted and stared at the girl who had, in only a few days, become both a fascination and the bane of his existence.

"Casanova, you are not," he said, barely suppressing a laugh.

Caleb thought about throwing Eli in the water for that remark but decided against it. He had enough trouble dealing with a girl who ran away from him at every turn. One who ran straight to Dan, their new brother. There were going to be repercussions there. Caleb had a sinking sensation that Eli stood no chance against the bond Dan and Mattie shared. He stood watching them laugh. There was such an easy camaraderie. You could see how much they cared. The two of them were tied together so tightly nothing would break them apart, maybe not even death.

"Think about your own problems before you give me relationship advice." Caleb peeled off his soaking wet shirt and wrung it out. He tossed it on board and then followed Eli to where Ava was sunning herself.

"Move over, Sissy." Caleb grinned at Eli's use of their nickname for her. Neither of them had used it in a while.

"Your girlfriend is not nice." Ava glared at where Mattie and Mary were lying.

"She's not normally like that," Eli said. "She was fine before we came out of the trees, and then it was like she did a complete one-eighty. I don't know what happened."

"Moody B."

"*Ava!*" Eli laughed. "You'll like her, I promise. She's pretty cool when she's not snarling at you."

"I like Mary, though," Ava said. "She's really nice, and she thinks Caleb's cute."

"Then why did she throw him in the lake?" Eli asked.

41

"Because he probably deserved it," Ava said with a grin.

"I'm right here, you know," Caleb grouched.

"We know," they sing-songed together.

Caleb tuned out their good-natured ribbing and lay back on the grass to let his jeans dry out. She actually had the nerve to throw him in the water. A laugh burst out. He couldn't help it. Mary wasn't like any girl he'd ever met.

"Is he okay?" Ava asked worriedly. "He's laughing."

"Have you guys seen Mattie?" Dan stood in front of them, his eyes scanning the surroundings.

"No. Did you check the boat?" Eli jumped up, his own eyes roaming.

"First thing I did. Mary's asleep. Mattie was too, but now she's gone."

"She can't be far," Caleb said, sitting up himself. "She was just here."

"Mattie!" Eli called out, but silence was his only answer.

Caleb saw Mary had roused. Eli's shout would have woken the dead. She sat up and rubbed her eyes. Dan motioned her over, and she stood, walking slowly. Caleb thought maybe her limp was bothering her more than she wanted to admit. They were on the water, and it had to be bothering the stiff joints she was sure to have.

"What's going on?" she asked once she reached them.

"Mattie's MIA." Dan sighed. "That girl is going to be the death of me yet."

"Can't Eli use his Mattie GPS and find her?"

Mary questioned.

Eli let out a snarl. "No. I've been trying, but I've got nothing. It's like she's not here. She's not anywhere."

"That can't be at all good, if you can't sense her," Ava said, stating the obvious.

Caleb closed his eyes and focused. When he opened them, he looked first at Eli. The connection between him and Mattie was there, but faint and a little broken. It went nowhere. Wherever she was, he couldn't reach. Then he looked at Dan. His link with Mattie was bright, glowing like a sun. It led into the woods. Caleb sucked in a breath. What did this mean? The Guardian Angel bond was the strongest that could be forged, but for some reason, Dan's was stronger.

"Dan." Caleb stood. "Close your eyes and think about Mattie. Just think about her and start walking."

Eli shot him a questioning look, but he only shook his head. Now was not the time to get into something he didn't understand himself.

Dan didn't argue, he just did what Caleb asked. Within a minute he started walking the same path as the bright light connecting him to Mattie.

"Eli, you and Ava go with him. Mary and I will check the opposite direction."

Caleb knew Dan would find her, but he wanted a chance to apologize to Mary without everyone around. If Eli needed him, he'd send him a text. Ava shot him a knowing look he ignored, but she ran after Dan and Eli. Mary looked none too pleased to be stuck with him.

"Let's go," she muttered and started walking. "What happened? She just walked off into the woods?"

"We're not sure. She was asleep beside you, and then she wasn't. None of us saw her walk away."

"That's weird, even for Mattie."

Caleb had to agree. It was downright odd. It was like she disappeared into thin air. Then again, her father's family seemed to have that same ability. It was part of why they'd never been caught by law enforcement. They seemed to simply vanish from the scene of the crime. Maybe she'd be able to shed some light on that particular ability.

They walked in silence for a few minutes, occasionally shouting Mattie's name, but Caleb knew they were walking in the wrong direction.

"Let's stop here for a few minutes," Caleb suggested after Mary stumbled for the tenth time. "Get our bearings."

Mary nodded gratefully and leaned against a tree. She looked around, her expression worried. "I hope she's all right. She always seems to get herself into some dangerous messes."

"Did you worry about that before inviting her to live with you?"

Mary smiled ruefully. "She could have super-secret ninjas beating down our door every night and I wouldn't care. Mattie is the reason I'm here, alive and well, and that is all that mattered to me. She's my sister now."

"And your mom?"

"Mom decided Mattie needed a home where she could be loved and accepted for who she is. She worries about Mattie's penchant for trouble, and she's had to accept a lot of strange stuff like ghost-proofing the house. My mom's religious, but all the stuff she's had to deal with recently...I think it's tested the limits of her beliefs."

"You seem to accept it without reservations." Caleb stared down into her earnest blue eyes and took a step closer to her.

"I had to either accept the supernatural or accept the fact I went crazy. Out of body experiences, hearing ghosts..." She shook her head. "What would you rather believe? Ghosts are real or you're crazy in the head?"

Caleb laughed. She had a point. "You're not crazy."

"That's what I tell myself daily."

"I'm sorry, Mary." Caleb stepped closer. "I didn't mean to hurt your feelings earlier. I was just worried you'd get hurt."

"You pissed me off," she corrected him.

"I'm sorry for that too." He gave her a strained smile. "I am arrogant sometimes without even realizing it. My mom says it's my worst flaw."

"It is," Mary agreed. "You shouldn't make assumptions about things you know nothing about."

"What I know is you are a strong, beautiful girl who shouldn't have had to suffer what you did. It didn't break you, though. I can see that every time you smile. It's full of happiness, despite what happened to you."

"Yes, well..." she muttered, looking down.

He put a finger under her chin and lifted her head up so she was looking at him. "Don't do that."

"What?"

"Look away and deflect attention from yourself. I've seen you do it all day."

"I don't like attention."

"Why?"

"Because I'm not beautiful anymore," she whispered. "I'm scarred and ugly."

Looking into her bruised expression, it felt like someone had punched him in the gut. Did she really think that?

"Mary, why would you think that? I think you're the most beautiful girl I've ever met."

"You haven't seen my scars."

"They're just scars," he said. "They don't define you unless you let them."

"Easy for you to say," she muttered.

"Mary, when I look at you, I see the warmth of the sun. I see laughter in your eyes, joy in your smile. I see the way you give your heart to the people you love. I see gentleness in you. I see strength and passion. I can see the purity of your soul. You're beautiful, and anyone who doesn't see that doesn't deserve you."

Her eyes widened when he stepped even closer. He leaned in, his lips brushing hers softly. She went still, and he teased her lips again, coaxing them to respond. His hand slid into her hair, tilting her head more, and he felt her give in, felt her lips slide against his. Emotions surged through him like a landslide, and for the first time in his life, he was helpless to move away from a woman.

His phone buzzed, and he ignored it for a moment, but then he remembered Mattie and tore himself away from Mary, reaching into his pocket. She looked at him, dazed, her face flushed. He grinned at her, looking at the text on his phone. The grin wilted as he read the text. Mattie had discovered the burial site of a serial killer.

That girl. Dan was right. She was going to be the death of them all.

"We need to go," he said grimly and showed Mary the text.

Mary nodded, a blush still coloring her cheeks. "Leave it to Mattie to find something like that."

Caleb shook his head, grabbed her hand, and started backtracking. She could get mad at him if she wanted to, but if she fell, he was going to catch her. Thankfully, she didn't object, and he just enjoyed the feel of her skin against his as they returned to the boat. They were in for a long day ahead. The police would have all kinds of questions.

At least Mary wasn't mad at him anymore. Or at least he hoped she wasn't.

Chapter Four

Mary knocked on the door promptly at six. She glanced over to her house. Mattie still wasn't home. She'd gone to visit her father today, and then she said she had to go to the DMV. That was an adventure in and of itself. No one went to the madhouse that was the Charlotte DMV office unless forced into it. Mary would rather go to a dentist than the DMV.

Mrs. Flynn opened the door, looking harried, a sippy cup in one hand. "Oh, thank God. Noah is hungry, and I still have to get into my dress. Can you feed him, please, Mary?"

Mary took the cup from her. "Yes. You go get dressed. Just show me the nursery."

The nursery was upstairs next to the master bedroom. It was decorated in soft tones of beige and tan, animal stickers on the walls. The crib and changing table were white, and a matching rocking chair sat in one corner. Noah stood in the crib, big tears falling down his baby cheeks as he cried. Mary wanted to just coo at him, he was so cute.

"Hey there, little man," she said as she approached him. "Do you remember me? I'm Mary."

His chubby little hands reached for the cup, and Mary laughed, handing it over. It went right to his mouth. It was only then that he looked up at her. Noah's eyes were bright from crying, but they were curious too. She ruffled his hair, and he leaned into her touch. He was such a beautiful baby with that curly mop of black hair and those sky blue eyes. This kiddo was going to be a heartbreaker when he got older.

"You and I are gonna get along just fine, little man," she whispered and tweaked his nose. He giggled, causing her to grin. Babies always made her happy. They were so innocent and hadn't yet learned what it was to hate or to hurt others. They were simply happy to have people love them.

"Thank you, Mary. We're running so late. Having a baby is taking us some time to adjust to."

Mary turned around to see Mr. Flynn standing in the doorway. He looked as tired as his wife. Noah must really be keeping them up.

"No worries," she said. "You should have called, and I would have come over earlier. I wouldn't have minded. Noah is a sweetheart."

A look Mary couldn't identify crossed his face, but she didn't think he had the same opinion of the baby as she did. Maybe it was just the lack of sleep. Getting used to a baby could take a lot of adjustments.

"He gets very fussy once he goes down," Mr. Flynn warned her. "He might get up several times."

"Mrs. Flynn told me." Mary glanced at Noah, who was happily sucking on his sippy cup. How could anyone not love that little face? "She also said the other sitters had some problems?"

The shuttered look that claimed his expression spoke volumes to Mary. Something had happened, but he was hoping it wouldn't again.

"It was nothing, really," he said, shrugging it off. "Noah cries a lot at night. I think they just couldn't handle it. Spooked them a bit."

Spooked? How could a baby crying spook someone? Frustrate them, yes, but not spook them.

"Here you are, Anthony." Mrs. Flynn pushed her husband out of the doorway and came over to place a kiss on Noah's head. He grinned up at her. The boy obviously already loved his new mama, and the feeling was mutual. Even tired and worn out, the woman was thankful for her child. They'd been trying for years to adopt, and Mary was so happy for her.

"You be good for Mary," she told Noah. "Please."

Mary gave her a reassuring smile. "I'm sure we'll be fine."

Mrs. Flynn ushered them all out of the nursery and downstairs. "Noah goes down at around seven thirty. He should be out by eight. Our numbers are posted on the fridge, which you are welcome to dive into if you get hungry or thirsty. I stocked it with soda earlier."

"Thanks, Mrs. Flynn."

Mary walked them out and locked the door. Then she went back upstairs. She paused outside Noah's door and listened. Nothing. Maybe she'd been wrong the other day at the park. There was no whispering going on now. She found the baby sitting in his crib, playing with a stuffed toy car.

"Ready to go downstairs, little man?" She reached in and picked him up. Mrs. Flynn had told her mother he was just a little over two years old, but he didn't talk a lot. The social worker said he'd been shuffled through two homes before the Flynn's adopted him. Poor little guy. She changed him into a pair of pajamas and made sure he was dry. He had on a diaper, but wore Pull-Ups during the day. Going through so many homes had caused him to not be potty trained yet. Mrs. Flynn was working on it, though.

"How about some SpongeBob?" she asked him as she carried him downstairs. "He's one of my favorites."

The TV remote took some finding. It was wedged in one of the couch cushions, but once she found it, she settled herself and Noah down to watch SpongeBob and Patrick torment Squidward. The baby laughed and cooed at the cartoon. She knew he'd love it. Everyone loved the Sponge that was Bob.

She pulled out her Kindle and opened her newest book, *The Ghost Host* by DelSheree Gladden. She'd started it last night. Having a foster sister who could see ghosts had made her buy the book, as the main character had the same gift. Maybe not the best book to be reading at the moment, considering she thought there was something spooky going on in the house, but she couldn't resist diving back into

Echo's world.

As the hour passed, Noah got sleepier and sleepier. She saw his little head start to fall, and he caught himself, trying to keep his sleepy eyes glued to the TV. She smiled and gently pulled him into her side so he was lying on her. He could fall asleep without falling over. She stroked his hair while they watched SpongeBob, and she hummed her favorite lullaby for him.

When she was sure he was sound asleep, she picked him up and took him to the nursery. He never moved as she tucked him in and turned on his nightlight. Mary stood for a moment and listened again, but there wasn't a whisper of a sound. Maybe she really had imagined whispering in the park.

Going back downstairs, she stopped by the kitchen to grab a soda out of the fridge. The faucet was on, a slow stream steadily falling. The Flynns must not have shut it off earlier when they were in here. Mary turned the faucet off and crinkled her nose. The most godawful scent wafted up from the sink. She fanned the air in front of her, trying to dispel it. Maybe the garbage disposal was backed up. She made a mental note to tell the Flynns when they got back. It needed to be dealt with as soon as possible. Theirs had backed up last summer, and Mary remembered the stench that had invaded the house for days after it was fixed.

Mrs. Flynn had stocked the fridge with Mountain Dew and Coke. Mary grabbed the Mountain Dew and snagged a bag of chips from the pantry. She went back to the living room, making sure the baby monitor was turned on so she could hear Noah. She snuggled down in the overly soft couch, turned the TV off, and started reading again.

A faint noise from the baby monitor caught her attention a little while later. She picked it up and pulled it closer to her ear. There. It sounded like something scratching. It wasn't static. This sounded like someone physically scratching at the wall.

Mary got up, holding the monitor, and walked toward the stairs to go and check on Noah. He wasn't crying, but the scratching was getting louder.

A child's laugh floated through the air, and Mary whirled, looking over the living room and into the kitchen. The Flynns had an open floor plan. There wasn't anywhere to hide, no hallways or anything on the main floor. Just a main floor powder room, the door open. No one was hiding in there.

She knew she heard a laugh, though. The scratching continued on the monitor. She'd look around down here after she checked on Noah. She ran up the stairs and into his room. He was sleeping, the nightlight off. Okay, Mary knew for a fact she'd turned that light on.

Movement to her left caused her to turn, and she sucked in her breath at what she saw. A shadowy figure sat hunched in the corner. It was small, like a child, but wrapped in darkness and shadows. It looked up, eyes burning a bright yellow. Mary took a step back, her hand clutching the crib railing, as her other hand dropped the baby monitor and fumbled to turn on the lamp. When she finally managed it, and bright light lit up the room, the shadow child was gone.

What in God's name was going on?

No way was she leaving Noah up here alone. She scooped him up, and he mumbled in his sleep. She held him tight as she inched out of the room and took him back downstairs. The Flynns had a Pack 'n Play in the living room, and she put Noah in there. Then she turned on all the lights and checked the time on the Time Warner Cable box. It was a little after ten. The Flynns would be home in two hours.

Then she was *making* Caleb listen to her. Something was wrong here.

Her phone rang, and she let out a shriek, not expecting the loud ringtone in the silence of the living room. She let out a nervous laugh and grabbed it from where she'd left it on the table. Mattie. Finally. Mary was dying to hear how her visit with her uber-scary dad went.

"Hey, Mattie. Why are you *only* just now calling me?"

"It's Caleb."

Why was Caleb calling her from Mattie's phone?

"We're all at the hospital. I told your mom I'd call, but I didn't have your number, so I borrowed Mattie's phone."

"What's wrong?" Dread curled in the pit of her stomach. Mattie was always getting herself into situations that caused her to be seriously injured. What had happened this time?

"There was an incident," he said softly. "Dan's in the hospital. It doesn't look good, and Mattie's shut down. She's not talking to anyone, and we can't get her to leave Dan's side. She needs you."

Mary felt like she'd been hit. Dan meant more to Mattie than anyone, even her. If it was as bad as

Caleb was making it out to be, Mattie would be devastated. She'd lost so much already. She couldn't lose Dan too.

"I'm babysitting," she murmured, shock starting to set in. "I…I can't leave."

"Can you call and see if they can come home early?" Caleb asked, his voice grim.

"Of course. I'll call, and then see if my mom can pick me up, I guess."

"I'll come get you," Caleb told her. "Where are you?"

"Across the street. I'm babysitting for my neighbor."

"I'm on my way."

Mary stared down at the phone when he hung up. Dan was hurt? How? He wasn't even on active duty. He'd taken time off to deal with everything going on with his mom and the Malones. Did it have something to do with Mattie and the ghost girls stalking her? She'd blame herself if it did.

Sighing, she got up and went to the kitchen to find Mrs. Flynn's cell phone number. She hated to do it to them, but this was a family emergency. She turned the water off as she waited for her to pick up her cell.

Why was the water on? She'd turned it off.

"Hello, Mary?" Mrs. Flynn's voice came over the line. "Is everything okay?"

"No, no it's not," she said, frowning at the faucet.

"What's wrong with Noah?" The panic in Mrs. Flynn voice snapped her back to the conversation.

"Noah's fine," she assured his mother. "I just got

55

a call, and I need to go to the hospital. There's a family emergency. I hate to ask, but is there any way you guys can come home a little early? I need to get there as soon as possible."

"Oh, sweetie, I hope everything is okay."

"I don't know yet. I just got a call to go to the hospital. It's Mattie and Dan."

"Your foster sister and that young policeman?" Mrs. Flynn asked.

"Yes, ma'am."

"Let us say goodbye, and we'll be straight home, honey. How is Noah? I was getting ready to call and check on him."

"He's fine," Mary murmured. "He's been asleep since a little after seven."

"He hasn't woken up at all?" Surprise colored Mrs. Flynn's voice.

"No. I did hear something on the monitor earlier. Noah was asleep when I checked on him, but I brought him downstairs with me in case the baby monitor wasn't working properly. He's passed out in the Pack 'n Play."

"Okay, Mary. We'll be there soon."

Mary put her phone in her back pocket and inspected the sink. It wasn't dripping, so why had it been on? She'd turned it off when she was in here earlier.

Footsteps sounded behind her, but she didn't turn this time. Instead she listened. They ran back and forth across the living room. They were small, the footsteps of a child. She turned ever so slightly so she could look at the crib out of the corner of her eye, but she saw nothing. She heard the whispering, though, the same whispering she'd heard in the park. And the smell was back, assaulting her in waves. It smelled like rotten eggs, making her gag.

She ran over to the playpen and picked the baby up, holding him. Her gaze darted around the room, but she saw nothing. Why, oh why, wasn't she like Mattie and able to see these things?

"Hello?" she whispered, her hand gently patting Noah's back to keep him asleep. "I can hear you whispering."

Silence answered her. She felt the temperature start to cool down. Her eyes narrowed. This wasn't a ghost. That much she knew from talking with Eli. Ghosts ran cold all the time, not just when the mood suited them. This thing was trying to fool her.

"You're not a ghost," she said, "so stop trying to pretend you are."

The room didn't get any colder, but it didn't warm back up either.

"Who are you?" The voice slithered into her ear, and she jumped, nearly screaming. Its voice sounded like smooth, silky velvet, which made it that much scarier. It could seduce, beguile, and Mary cringed away from it. This thing was dangerous.

The stench kept her grounded. It was awful. It clustered at the back of her throat, making it almost impossible to breathe.

"Who are you?" she countered. Never tell them your name. It was the only thing all the internet sites she'd read agreed on. Names were powerful.

It chuckled, and she felt it against her back, the hot, putrid breath on her neck. She got the distinct impression it was sniffing her, and she shuddered in horror.

A child's laugh rang out, startling Mary. What was this thing? What did it want with Noah?

The doorbell rang and she did scream, waking Noah up. He started to cry.

"*Mary!*"

She let out a sigh of relief, recognizing Caleb's voice. She didn't think twice, just ran for the door. It took her a minute, but she got the deadbolt unlocked and ripped it open. She saw Caleb's eyes widen, but she guessed the panic and the fear must be plastered across her face.

"What's wrong?" he demanded, pushing his way in.

"There was something here," she said. "I think it wants the baby."

Noah was crying, and Mary shifted him, trying to soothe him. Maybe he could see whatever it was. "Easy, little man," she shushed. "Nothing is gonna get you while Mary's got you."

"Tell me what's going on." Caleb closed the door and took a quick look around.

Mary ignored him, focusing on Noah. He was scared and clutching her like she was the last life vest on a sinking boat. His big blue eyes were wide with fear, and she cradled him as best she could and started to hum as she rocked him.

Caleb walked upstairs, clearly realizing she wasn't going to do anything until she calmed Noah down. Mary was relieved he was here. At least if something was still present, he would see it.

It took her nearly fifteen minutes to calm Noah,

and then another ten to get him back to sleep. She didn't want to put him in the playpen again, so she held him. When she heard the key in the lock, Caleb stood from his position on the couch. The Flynns came in, looking from her to Caleb.

"This is Caleb Malone," she introduced, keeping her voice quiet so as not to wake Noah. "He came to take me to the hospital."

"Malone?" Mr. Flynn looked at Caleb thoughtfully. "James Malone's son?"

"Yes, sir." Caleb nodded.

"I've met your father a time or two," Mr. Flynn said. "Good man."

"You know my dad?" Caleb's eyebrows shot up.

Mr. Flynn gave him a rueful smile. "We've called him on a case or two when I was a detective in Chicago."

Maybe Mr. Flynn wouldn't be so opposed to thinking something was in the house, then, if he knew Caleb's dad, who worked the Spook Squad in the FBI.

"We need to get going, Mary."

Mary handed the sleeping baby to his father. "Don't put him the nursery by himself. Keep him in your room tonight."

He gave her a questioning look. "Trust me, Mr. Flynn. Keep him with you tonight."

Before he could ask any more questions, she grabbed her purse and fled the house, grateful to be out of there. She was seriously spooked. And she needed to know what was going on with Dan and Mattie. Caleb could explain it on the way to the hospital, and she'd tell him about what happened at the Flynns'.

Chapter Five

Caleb leaned against the doorway watching Mattie sit at his brother's bedside. Her face was white, her eyes bruised and haunted. Eli hovered in the background, looking worried and helpless. It was a feeling they were all experiencing. They'd just found Dan, and now, if the doctors were right, they were going to lose him. It had been three days since they'd admitted him for head trauma. He wasn't on life support, but his brain activity was slowly dying. He was dying.

His brother was dying.

What should he feel? If it were Eli lying there, he'd be beside himself, but he and Eli grew up together. Dan was new, both of them trying to feel each other out. He was sad, upset, and his heart ached for Mattie, and the Richards family, but he didn't love Dan like he did Eli, Benny, or Ava. And that was the reason he felt so guilty.

Mattie made a nonsense sound, and he swung his eyes back to her. She looked beaten and broken all at once. She made that weird keening noise sometimes. He'd heard it once before when he was about nine. A woman his dad was helping ended up losing her husband. He'd watched her hold the man and make that same sad noise. That was the first time he'd seen an aura. The emotion had been so intense, it had awakened his gift. The bright blue light had lit them up until his aura died out. The bond between them snapped and that was when the noise had been torn from her. She'd felt his death. His mom had explained that she had loved her husband since they were children. She'd been the other half of his heart and his soul.

Caleb suspected this was the case between Mattie and Dan, even if neither of them recognized it.

Eli was beginning to see what Caleb saw too. He'd watched the knowledge dawn upon Eli as they'd all sat around waiting for Dan's condition to change. It was the look on her face, in her eyes. The way she sat hunched over, refusing to move, eat, or speak. She hadn't said a word to anyone since they'd brought him in. Even Mary couldn't get her to talk. If Dan died, she'd never get over it.

His father had told him the demon, Silas, had used Dan as a guinea pig for a demon spell he wanted to use on Mattie. The spell wasn't what put him in a coma. It was the head injury he'd sustained in the process. From what his dad had said, Mattie had forced Silas to protect Dan from the reaper trying to take him. Silas had hidden him, even from Mattie. She was helpless to do anything but sit and watch and pray.

Anger bled through Caleb. Rage ate at him the

more he thought about a demon using his brother as a science experiment. He wanted to blame Mattie, but he couldn't. He should blame her, but the magic in his blood designed him to protect her, a living reaper on Earth. It wouldn't *let* him blame her.

His father tapped him on the shoulder and motioned him to come outside. Caleb followed him to the waiting room. James Malone looked as haggard as Dan's adoptive father did. It was different for him. He'd loved Dan while their mother was pregnant with him. James had mourned him, rejoiced when he found out he was alive, and was now contemplating losing him again. It just wasn't fair. To any of them.

"This situation with Mary's neighbor, is it serious?" His dad ran a hand through his hair. "Or can it wait a few days?"

"I think it can wait. From what she said, it sounds like the early stages of infestation."

"Demons." Disgust rolled off James's tongue.

"Yes. It's only in the first stages—odors, scratching at the walls, the faucets turning on and off, things like that."

"She thinks it's attached itself to the child?"

Caleb sat down, his brow furrowed. "When I first met the boy, it was the day we all went to the police station. He was with his mother in the park across the street. What caught my attention was the fact that he had two shadows."

"Two?"

"Yeah, I had that dumbfounded look on my face too." A faint smile appeared. "I still don't understand it. I've never seen any creature or demon that can do that."

"I need to do some research on it," James said. "Don't do anything until I tell you to. We need to know what we're dealing with."

His father didn't have to tell him twice. He and Eli had once gone out and hunted a demon without researching it. They'd both nearly died that night. If their dad hadn't saved their butts, neither of them would be here.

"I'm going to take your mother and Benny home. They're tired. Will you call if anything changes?"

Caleb nodded. "Yeah, I'll sit out here with Ava. She's dead on her feet, and I don't want to leave her alone in the waiting room."

"How is he?" Ava asked as soon as their father disappeared around the corner.

Caleb glanced over, surprised she was awake. He'd assumed she'd passed out. "He's getting worse."

A tear slipped down her cheek. She'd been so excited for a new brother, but that was Ava. She'd loved him from the moment their father had told her. Didn't matter if Dan returned her love or not. She had enough for both of them.

"It'll be okay, Sissy." Caleb moved and sat down beside her, wrapping an arm around her hunched shoulders. "Remember what Mom always says. When it's our time to go, then we've served our purpose, and we can die peacefully knowing we did good things on this Earth."

"It shouldn't be his time," she railed. "We just found him."

"It's not fair."

They both glanced up to see Mr. Richards, Dan's father, standing across from them. He looked so exhausted, worse even than their own father.

"I wish you'd gotten to know him. He was such a good kid, always helping people. He loved his family more than almost anything in the world."

"Don't forget Mattie," Ava reminded him, her gaze wandering to the door leading to Dan's room.

A hollow chuckle slipped out of Mr. Richards. "Dan loves that girl more than anyone in this world, and I know Mattie loves my son. You can't pry her away from him. I thought she was going to commit homicide when his mother told him it was all right to let go. If there is any hope of him coming out of this, my bets are resting on Mattie. If anyone can will Dan back, it's her."

"I hope you're right," Ava whispered.

"So do I," Mr. Richards said. "I have to get my wife home before our little ragamuffin in there sees her again."

Caleb watched him walk away, his face having aged ten years since he'd seen the man at the police station a few days ago. Blood or not, he was Dan's father. No one would ever take that from either of them.

Mary came around the corner, and Caleb jumped up. Ava giggled, and he shot her a glare. He'd been thinking about their kiss all day.

"You headed home?" he asked when she slowed down, seeing them.

"Yeah." She rolled her shoulders, trying to relieve the pressure. "I'm taking Mom's car home.

She still has another six hours on shift."

"I'll walk you to your car," Caleb offered, herding her toward the elevator, ignoring Ava's laughter. Thankfully, Mary was too tired to pay attention to it.

The elevator ride down to the main floor consisted of Mary yawning and Caleb watching the floor numbers change. He fidgeted and kept peeking at her out of the corner of his eye. When the doors dinged open, he almost jumped. Shaking his head, he followed the subdued ray of sunshine out of the elevator and into the brightly lit main floor.

By the time they reached Mrs. Cross's car, Caleb felt hot and sweaty. He wanted to say something, but he was tongue-tied. Never happened to him before. His mother adored her, and it made him nervous.

"Thanks for walking me down." She turned those sleepy blue eyes up at him, and he swallowed thickly.

"No problem."

"Well, I guess I should go..." She stared pointedly at him. He leaned against the car door, not only for support, but to keep her from driving away.

"I wanted to ask you something." An idea was forming.

She raised her eyebrows curiously.

"There's this thing Saturday night," he said. "It's the Policemen's Ball. Dad is making me and Eli go. Well, only if Dan pulls through. None of us is leaving until we know something."

He was babbling, and she was looking like she wanted to shove him out of her way and drive off.

"Anyway, I was thinking you might like to go...with me."

"You're asking me out on a date?"

"No...well, yeah, I guess. I was a jerk, and I wanted to make it up to you. So I thought you might want to go to the ball."

"So it's not a date?" She looked dubious.

"No...maybe...I don't know."

A look his mother often gave Eli when he was frustrating her crossed Mary's face, and he winced. That wasn't a good thing.

"Well, Caleb, when you figure it out, I'll let you know. Now move so I can go home and get some sleep."

Caleb moved at the anger in her voice. Great. He'd gone and mucked that up worse than the last time she'd been mad at him. He watched her drive off, feeling like a bumbling fool. No help for it; he'd made an idiot of himself.

He closed his eyes and shook his head before going back inside to check on Dan and then sit with Ava. All they could really do now was wait and see what happened.

***

Mary yawned and answered her phone on the third ring. "Mmm...hello?"

"Hi, Mary, it's Thalia Flynn."

Mary rubbed her eyes and sat up, coming awake at the sound of the woman's voice. "Hi, Mrs. Flynn."

"Did I wake you?" she fretted. "I know you've

all been at the hospital with that young man."

"It's fine." Mary glanced at the clock. 9:45 a.m. She'd gotten to bed late last night, sitting up and talking with Mattie.

"How is he?"

"He pulled through," Mary told her, stifling another yawn. She still didn't know all the details, but whatever had brought Dan back was some powerful juju. She snorted at her own thought. Yup, way too many episodes of *Supernatural* for her.

"That's wonderful!" Mrs. Flynn sounded genuinely pleased.

"Did you need something, Mrs. Flynn?" she asked, deciding to hurry this along. She might get in a few more hours of sleep.

"Yes." She actually heard her take a deep breath. "Noah seems to get on with you so well. He wasn't at all fussy with you, was he?"

"No." Mary shoved her feet into her slippers. The need to pee was becoming urgent. "He slept most of the night."

"He hasn't taken to any of the other sitters." Mrs. Flynn's words were rushed. "Anthony has to work. They just found the third child who has gone missing in the Charlotte area this morning. He'll be cloistered with the police force all day and most of the night. I need to go out tonight. I made plans for a function that I can't miss, especially with Anthony's promotion…"

"It's cool, Mrs. Flynn," Mary interrupted her before she went any further. "I'd be happy to watch Noah for you." She'd just call Caleb if she needed help. She made sure to put his number in her phone when they were at the hospital.

"Oh, thank you!"

Mary laughed and promised to be there by seven. She ran to the bathroom once she hung up and let out a long sigh of relief. Trying to hold it when you first woke up was not advised. After she'd washed her hands, she peeked in Mattie's room, finding her stumbling around in six-inch heels. The girl looked like she was gonna break her neck. Mary went to her closet and found the answer to Mattie's prayers.

"You've never worn heels before, have you?" Mary asked, a laugh bubbling out as she watched Mattie wobble on the heels.

"Yes, I *have* worn heels before!" Mattie all but yelled. "Just not six-inch heels. God, this is torture."

"Did you buy a second pair of shoes that aren't so high?"

"Have you ever gone clothes shopping with Meg?" she asked dryly. "It's very unpleasant, and once she found out I had a credit card with no limit..." Mattie shook her head in disgust. "She went nuts making me try on dresses."

Mary laughed at Mattie's surly tone. "Well, then, I guess it's a good thing I still have *my* shoes from last year's Christmas formal, isn't it?"

"You have shoes?" Mattie turned and fell headfirst onto the carpet. She ripped the shoes off and tossed them aside. "Where?"

"Two-inch heels." She pulled the shoes from behind her back and tossed them to the panicked girl. "Think you can stay upright in those?"

The black, strappy heels fit her perfectly, and she could not only stand, but walk with a barely discernable wobble. "Perfect, Mary! Thank you so much!"

"So how did shopping with the backstabber go?" Mary asked, flopping down on Mattie's bed.

"It was nice."

"That bad, huh?"

Her sigh filled the entire room. "Can we not talk about it?"

"Sure thing."

"So are you accepting Caleb's invite to the ball tomorrow night?" Mattie asked, falling beside her on the bed.

"Why should I?" Mary grumbled. "He's only doing it because he wants to apologize for being an ass."

"That's true, but why let that stop you from going to the 'party of the year,' as Meg calls it? Go have fun, dance with some *very* cute cops."

Mary sighed. Caleb had asked her to the dance while they were in the hospital. It felt more like a pity date than anything else. She was not a girl to be pitied.

"Look, go show him that just because he's blind, doesn't mean everyone else is. How's Caleb ever going to see you if you don't show him what he's missing? Besides, you might meet someone who puts Caleb to shame."

Mary gaped at her. The girl was crazy if she thought anyone could put Caleb Malone to shame. "Oh my God, have you seen his abs? I don't think there's *anyone* who can put him to shame."

"The point is to make him jealous, Mary. Who cares if the other guys have better abs or not?"

"I don't have a dress," she said. "And no shoes, now that you have mine."

"Ah, but I have a credit card with no limit," Mattie reminded her. "I can buy you a dress and a new pair of shoes."

"Mattie, you hate having that card," Mary argued. "Just the thought of using it almost makes you hyperventilate."

"Spending it on myself does that," she qualified. "Spending it on you? Different story altogether."

"I call BS," Mary said. "You absolutely hate even looking at it. I think you'd cut it up and flush it if you could."

"Okay, I'll admit I don't like the money my father is doing his best to foist upon me, but that doesn't mean I can't buy you a dress and shoes. It'll make me feel better if I spend it on other people, anyway."

Mary stared at her foster sister and thanked God for the thousandth time he'd brought Mattie into their lives. The girl was one of the most unselfish people she'd ever met. A soft laugh escaped her lips. "You try so hard to pretend to be tough, but you're nothing but a big old softy."

"Bite your tongue!" Mattie scowled at her. "I am *not* a softy!"

Mary laughed harder at her outrage. Mattie sat up and grabbed her phone from where it was charging on the nightstand, putting Mary's danger sensors on red alert. Her laughter died as she narrowed her eyes at Mattie. What was she up to?

"Hey, Caleb, it's Mattie."

Mary's eyes widened in a kind of horrified

shock. *She did not!*

"Don't you dare," Mary mouthed at her.

Mattie ignored her. "Mary decided she wanted to go the party after all. Pick her up at seven tomorrow night."

Eyes wide and mouth open, Mary tried for a glare, but it just wasn't forming. She was too shocked.

"Because she's currently trying on dresses," Mattie answered whatever he'd asked. "I said I'd call while she figures out which lacy bra she wants to wear with her dress. It's really hard to find all the right accessories for a dress, wouldn't you say?"

Ohmygosh...she did *not* just say lacy bra?

"Yup. Seven on the dot. Don't be late." She disconnected the call.

"I am seriously going to murder you!" Mary threw a pillow at her head.

"Don't tell me I'm going soft again." She laughed before letting out a dramatic sigh. "When do you want to go shopping? We should probably go back to that little boutique where I got my dress. It has some nice stuff."

"Um, Mattie, I saw the price tag on your dress." Mary frowned. "Not sure I should let you buy something that expensive for me."

"You can't wear just anything," she told Mary. "It's a masquerade ball based on an old-fashioned cotillion. You have to have a specific type of dress for this party. That's the only place in town that sells them, so deal with it."

Mary did not feel comfortable letting Mattie spend that kind of money on her, even if she could afford it. It just didn't feel right, but she could tell Mattie wasn't going to take no for an answer.

"Give me an hour?" she asked, finally caving. "I need to shower and make sure we put dinner in the crockpot for tonight."

"Sure," Mattie agreed. "Come get me when you're ready."

Mary ran back to her room and dived into the closet, pulling out capris and a white tank top. She needed to shower quickly. She had to shop and still get back in time to babysit.

Chapter Six

Eli smacked Caleb in the head.

"Hey!" Caleb shouted at his brother, irritated.

"Get your head out of thoughts of Mary in lacy underwear. Dad wants to see us in the library."

Caleb groaned. Why, oh, why had he put that call on speakerphone? Eli had been teasing him all day. Not that he hadn't thought about Mary in lacy underwear...once the image was there, it just wouldn't go away. What he didn't need was Eli ribbing him about it.

Their father was on the phone when they came in. He put a finger to his lips when he saw them. They took a seat on the couch and waited. Caleb looked around, seeing books spread out across the massive table in the middle of the room. Curious, he got up and went over to examine them.

He noticed straightaway they were demon texts. He recognized the symbols on some of them. They were old, the covers a pure white that reeked of sulphur. What was his dad doing consulting demonic writing?

"Yes, yes, mayor. I understand. This will be handled." James paused. "Yes, sir, you have my word."

He closed his eyes and rubbed his head when he finally hung up. "We have a problem."

"When don't we?" Eli asked sardonically, earning himself a look of reprimand.

"This is serious, Eli. You've seen the reports of the missing children over the last few weeks? They just found the latest little girl this morning at a dump site."

"Okay?" Eli asked, curious.

Caleb was only half listening to the conversation. His entire focus was on the passage he was reading about the demon Deleriel. He was supposedly the first demon made, and the right hand of Lucifer himself. The demon fed off the souls of children.

"Caleb?"

"Hmm?" He kept reading, and his eyes widened. The demon would always pick one child whose soul shined brighter than the others and attach himself to him or her, feeding off the little one and growing stronger while the child grew weaker. The host could be determined when two shadows stalked the child.

"These murders aren't the work of an ordinary serial killer," James said. "They are the work of one of the most powerful demons to walk the Earth."

"Deleriel." Caleb finally looked up. "There isn't a way to stop him in this text."

"No." His father shook his head. "I think the little boy you were telling me about is his host. I also think we caught him in the early stages of his ownership."

"So what are we going to do?"

"First, I need to go see the mayor about the murders. Then I need to talk to the boy's father. I know him. We've worked a few cases together. He'll be open to what we'll need to do."

"What exactly do we need to do?" Caleb asked.

"Exorcise the demon from the child."

Caleb's eyes widened. They'd only seen their father perform one exorcism, and that had nearly broken him. He'd sat for weeks, desolate and haunted. This wasn't something to be taken on lightly, and if James Malone was suggesting it, things had to be dire.

***

Mary checked her watch again. 6:57 p.m. She'd just made it. For a while there, she was worried they wouldn't get home in time, but she needn't have feared. Mattie truly hated shopping. She'd rushed Mary through the whole process, earning her a few put out glares. Mary adored shopping, and being able to find a dress as beautiful as the blue concoction they'd found…she was in heaven. It hid her scars and made her look almost pretty again.

The door opened before she could knock. Mrs. Flynn looked relieved. Mary figured she thought she'd been stood up.

"I meant to get here earlier," Mary said, "but I had to go shopping for a dress for the Policemen's Ball. Sorry, Mrs. Flynn. I didn't mean to worry you."

"You're going to the masquerade tomorrow night?" Mrs. Flynn's eyes widened. Mary guessed she was going to hit her up to watch Noah for that event too.

"Yes." Mary smiled. "I'm excited."

Mrs. Flynn moved back, allowing Mary inside. "Noah's been fed and changed. He shouldn't be too hard to get down. I had him outside all day with me. He's played himself out, I think."

"Awesome." Mary held up her Kindle. "I've been catching up on all these books I download but never have time to read."

Mrs. Flynn picked up her purse and keys. "Don't hesitate to call if you need anything."

"No worries. We'll be all good."

Nodding, Mrs. Flynn let herself out, and Mary went to sit beside Noah on the floor. He was happily playing with some blocks.

"Hey, little man. Remember me?"

The toddler looked up at her, his eyes serious. Those baby blues of his shouldn't look like that. They should be happy and laughing. Instead they were haunted.

"Just you and me tonight, little man." She ruffled his hair. "Want to watch some SpongeBob?"

She found the cartoon and settled down, her back against the coffee table. Noah crawled to sit in her lap. He looked so tired. She stroked his baby soft hair, humming to the nonsense song SpongeBob was singing. Noah started to relax and was asleep within a few minutes. Poor baby.

Mary didn't move him. She adjusted him so he wasn't sleeping at an odd angle and let him lie there. She opened her Kindle and resumed where she left off reading *The Ghost Host*.

When she looked up, it was dark outside. The cable box told her it was half past nine. Wow. She'd finally finished the book and gotten herself a cramped neck in return. She rubbed at the sore muscle before picking Noah up and standing. She put him down in the Pack 'n Play, making sure the table lamp beside it was on. No shadows for him tonight.

She went foraging in the fridge and found a can of Mountain Dew. A bag of chips from the pantry completed her snack. The sink was behaving tonight as well. That was a good sign.

A *Supernatural* marathon was playing. Dean...*mmm*...every girl's dream guy. The poster of Dean, Sam, and Cass was one of two posters that adorned her wall at home. Mattie always teased her about it, but Mary knew for a fact the girl loved that show. One of Mary's favorite episodes about the Ghost Facers was playing. Seeing them running around in an old house, screaming at things they only talked about coming to life...comic relief at its best. She laughed so hard at one point, she almost spewed pop on the Flynns' white carpet.

A knock at the door startled her. She glanced at the time. 10:15 p.m. Who was knocking at this time of night? She put her drink down and went to the door, squinting through the peephole. She didn't see anyone, so she looked out the window, and the porch appeared empty.

The age-old horror movie question popped in her head. Should she open the door and investigate, or leave it alone? Someone had knocked, even if they weren't there now. So if she opened it, there might be some crazy person ready to hack her to pieces. Best to not open the door. Yeah, she didn't want to end up on the other side of Jason Voorhees's machete. She watched too many scary movies.

She checked on Noah and went to sit back down when a knock sounded at the back door. She froze. Had whoever knocked run around to the back door? Nervous, she crept over to the kitchen door and peered out through the glass pane. The Flynns had a curtain over it, but Mary would rather have a solid door. Especially right now.

Flipping on the back porch light, she let her gaze roam over the back yard. It looked empty, just the pool and the patio furniture. A loud knock pounded at the front door, and Mary's head swiveled in that direction. Someone was messing with her, and she didn't play games. Not after what happened to her. She yanked her cell out and called 911.

"This is the 911 dispatch. What is your emergency?"

"Someone is outside." Mary cut off the porch light and then turned off the kitchen lights. "They keep knocking on the doors and hiding."

"Have they tried to get in the house?"

"Not yet, but I think they might."

"What's your name?" the dispatcher asked and then took down her address as well. "I'm sending a patrol car to your house. Do you need me to stay on the phone until they—"

The call dropped. Mary groaned. At least the police were coming. She grabbed the butcher knife out of the knife block. Never again would she be weaponless.

Her mom was working, and Mattie was at the hospital with Dan. No quick help from either of them.

The banging started on the front door again. Louder and harder, it shook the door on its hinges. She inched closer, not daring to look outside. "I called the cops!" she shouted, and then shot a quick glance at Noah. He was still sleeping. How he could sleep through this, she didn't know.

She dialed Mrs. Flynn's number, but it went to voicemail. She left a message asking her to please call as soon as she heard the message, not telling her anything else. No need to panic her when the police would be here soon. Any police officer who worked this sector had to recognize the Flynns' name and address.

Tap...tap...tap.

What was that? Mary turned slowly, looking in all directions. The only sound was the TV playing quietly. Where had that come from?

Tap...tap...tap.

The window. Someone was tapping on the glass.

Her fingers found Caleb's number. He answered on the second ring. "Mary?"

"I need help," she whispered. "Someone's outside."

"Someone's trying to get in the house?" She could almost feel the instant alertness that came over him. "Did you call 911?"

"Yes, but I don't know how long it will take them to get here."

The knocking started again, this time at both the back and front doors. Mary's hand shook as memories of being kidnapped assaulted her. Of waking up, tied down to a chair, helpless and unable to move. Panic seized her.

"Mary, turn off all the lights. Make it hard for them to see you. I'm coming. Stay on the phone with me, okay?"

"Okay." She did what he said, even cutting off the lamp beside Noah's makeshift bed.

"Have you gone outside?"

"Do you think I'm stupid?" she snapped, her fear making her voice harsher than she'd meant. "I'm a horror movie fan. I know better than that." A chuckle sounded over the phone. "This is not funny, Caleb."

"I know, I'm sorry," he apologized. "When did this start?"

"A few minutes…" A scream was pulled from her when the loud banging started right on the wall she was leaning against. She jumped away, her eyes hunting the room.

"What happened?" Caleb demanded.

That was inside, not outside. Fear curled in the pit of her stomach. A small laugh echoed in the room, and Mary nearly collapsed. It wasn't someone messing with her. It was *something.*

"I don't think it's outside, Caleb," she whispered, moving to stand by Noah.

"They got in?" Alarm spiced Caleb's voice. "Mary get out, get out now."

"No, you don't understand." She fumbled for the light and finally got the lamp turned on, bathing

Noah in the soft white glow. He was still sleeping. "I think it wants Noah."

"Where are you?" She heard the dread in Caleb's voice.

"I'm babysitting Noah."

Footsteps on the stairs caught her attention. They were heavy, like that of a man. She turned to face the stairs, knife held out in front of her.

"Mary, get Noah and go to your house. Do it now. There are wards up there to protect against demons."

Mary reached down and awkwardly picked up the baby. He roused, his sleepy eyes looking up at her.

"Shh, baby. We're just going to go across the street to my house."

She all but ran to the door, unlocked it, and tried to open it. It wouldn't budge. She made sure the deadbolt and the doorknob lock weren't engaged. Neither were, but the door wouldn't budge. She held Noah tight and moved to the kitchen door. It wouldn't open either.

"Caleb, I don't think it's going to let us out."

"Why? What's wrong?"

"The doors won't open."

Fingers grazed her bare arm, and she whimpered, remembering when she'd been blindfolded. She felt fingers running over her skin, deciding where to hurt her. Tears leaked out of her eyes as the horror of those three weeks washed over her. "Please, not again," she whispered, her voice full of pain and dread.

"I'm coming, Mary. I swear."

She barely heard Caleb as the fear overwhelmed her. Her body shook when she felt those fingers ghosting over her arms, up her throat, down her hips. No…no…no…

The phone slipped from her fingers, and she cried, closing her eyes. Please, not again, please.

Noah's screaming jarred her enough to notice he was clutching her for dear life. Something was pulling at him. Trying to take him out of her arms.

"*No!*" she shouted and yanked him tighter to her, doing her best to quell the memories assaulting her. She couldn't let Noah get hurt.

That horribly beautiful laugh sounded in her head. "Mine," he whispered and ripped the baby away from her. Noah shrieked, terrified, and Mary tried to get him back, but then he was gone. Just gone.

No, where was he? Mary ran to the living room, turning on every light she could find. Noah was nowhere.

The crackling of the baby monitor sounded, and she whirled, snatching it up off the small table beside the couch. She could hear whispering, hear Noah softly crying. He had to be in the nursery. Turning for the stairs, she stopped when the walls started to shake, the pounding echoing throughout. Footsteps ran through the living room, like several children running.

Don't look, Mary told herself and grabbed the railing of the stairs. Her body suddenly felt like it was bogged down, heavy weights tied to her limbs. Her breath left her when she glanced up to the top of the stairs. That same small figure she'd seen in

Noah's room was crouched at the top, its glowing yellow eyes fixed on her.

It might have once been a child, but whatever it was now, it was full of hate and the need to hurt. Mary saw that in its eyes. It was guarding the way to Noah's room. This was one battle it wasn't winning. Mary fought her way up the stairs, the knife clutched in one hand.

Just as she reached the top step, tiny hands clutched handfuls of her hair, pulling her backward. Mary tumbled down the stairs, the knife she held sliding into the soft skin of her side. She cried out at the pain and lay still for a full minute before moving. She had to get to Noah.

That thought drove her to her feet, her hand pulling out the knife and throwing it aside. She ran for the staircase, but something grabbed her hair, then yanked and slammed her into the wall. Twice more her face got a full frontal up close and personal with the wall.

Noah screamed, and Mary groaned. She ran, ignoring the pain as her hair was ripped away from her scalp. She mounted the stairs, noting the thing at the top was gone, and she didn't feel like her legs were encased in lead. They were both in there with Noah. Once she hit the top of the stairs, she ran for the nursery, shoving the door open. There had been resistance, but her adrenaline was running so high she'd pushed right through. The baby sat in his crib, a massive dark figure hunched over him, doing…something.

Mary couldn't see what it was doing, but Noah was screaming for all he was worth. Whatever it was, it hurt. Not thinking about it, Mary ran straight for the crib, snatched up the baby, and then ran for the door.

She heard another pounding at the front door and people shouting. That thing stood by the stairs again. Mary knew it wouldn't let her near it. She turned and fled into the master bedroom, locking the door behind her. She dared not put Noah down.

Looking around, she saw the fireplace and the iron poker resting in its holder beside it. Iron. Iron was bad for the supernatural. She remembered from reading it on several sites, and the show *Supernatural* supported the theory. Couldn't hurt. She picked it up. It was surprisingly heavy for something so small.

The doorknob rattled.

Mary's nostrils flared, and she maintained a death grip on the poker.

A loud crash sounded downstairs as the bedroom door splintered inward. A figure stood there, well over six feet, draped in a dark hooded robe of some kind. Shadows cloaked it, and dozens of tiny childlike creatures clustered around its legs. Yellow glowing eyes stared at her, evil glaring at her from hate-filled expressions.

"*Mary!*"

She heard Caleb, but she couldn't take her eyes off all those children. This thing had done that to them, had turned them into this. Her heart broke. As terrified as she was, her heart still broke for these poor lost little souls. She wanted to cry at the horror of it. Pity filled her.

A snarl from the hooded creature brought her

eyes up. His eyes weren't yellow, but a dark amber color. They stared at her curiously. "You pity them even though they are going to devour you?"

"Yes," she told it, and the simple truth struck her. No matter what had happened to Mary, despite the horrors that had been visited upon her, she still kept her compassion for others, her heart bleeding for their pain.

"You are...curious." He took his hood off, and Mary gasped. She'd been expecting some dark, ugly monster. Instead, there stood a man who took her breath away. His strong features looked like they'd been sculpted by the angels themselves. He was beautiful. It was a deadly beauty, but it still caused her to stare. "I am Deleriel."

"Mary." The word slipped out, and she wanted to smack herself. Why had she told him her name?

"The mother of Christ's name," he murmured, his eyes hooding. "We have guests."

She could hear them coming up the stairs.

He walked over to her, his fingers tracing the curve of her face. "Curious, indeed. You aren't afraid of me."

And she wasn't. She was more afraid of those little creepy children in that moment.

"You can't have Noah." She wrapped her arms tighter around the little boy, who was whimpering, his face buried in her neck.

"You're strong, a fighter." Deleriel's hand cupped her cheek, and warm sensation washed over her face. "Keep the child. There are more I can harvest."

Harvest?

"Get away from her!"

Mary turned to see Caleb standing in the doorway. More footsteps pounded up the stairs.

"We will see each other again, little one," he whispered and then vanished.

"Where did he go?" Eli demanded, pushing his way into the room.

Mary's vision blurred a little, the sharp sting in her side reminding her of the wound. Her hand pressed against it, and when she pulled it away, blood covered it.

"Caleb, get the baby," she managed to get out before her vision darkened and she passed out.

***

Mary came awake a little while later, roused by the steady beeping of machines. She opened her eyes and saw she was in an emergency room hospital bed.

"Hey, sleepyhead."

Mary looked over to see Caleb sitting in a chair beside her. Why was she in the hospital, and why was Caleb here? It took her a moment, but then memories of the last few hours came rushing back, and her eyes widened.

"Noah?" The panic that filled her voice drove her to try to sit up. She gasped as the pain hit.

"Don't do that." Caleb gently pushed her back down. "Noah is fine. He's home with his parents."

"But…"

"Dad is taking care of it personally," Caleb assured her. "He's demon-proofing the house and placing a protection tattoo on the little boy. Eli is inking him as we speak."

"But that hurts…"

"There's a doctor who works on Dad's team over there too, and he put Noah out."

Mary let out a sigh of relief. Even if Deleriel broke his word and went back for Noah, he couldn't easily take him.

"Are you okay?"

Mary laughed. This was nothing. "I'm good. When can I go home?"

"As soon as the doctor clears you of any head trauma. You took a couple hits to your noggin."

"Well, my face took a few hits, but not my head."

"Are you sure?" Caleb asked. "That would leave bruises, Mary, and there aren't any bruises on your face."

Her hand went up to cup the same cheek Deleriel had. She'd felt an odd sensation when he'd done it. Had he healed her face?

"Maybe." Caleb nodded and then laughed at her startled expression. "It's easy to tell what you're thinking. You have the most open and honest face I've ever seen."

"Do you know anything about the demon who attacked us?" Mary asked, trying to divert his attention away from her.

Caleb shook his head, clearly understanding what she was doing. "Yeah, he's dangerous. You and Noah are lucky to have survived."

"Who is he?"

"The hand of Lucifer himself." Caleb hit the

nurse's call button. "Let's get you checked, and I'll tell you more tomorrow when you're feeling better, okay?"

She nodded and waited until the horde of nurses and doctors who came in were done examining her. Her mother bustled in as well, scared and pale, Mattie right behind her. Mary assured them both she was fine. Caleb had told her mother someone broke into the Flynns' house, and Mary had saved Noah. Mary wasn't sure what they'd said to the Flynns, and she was sure he'd told Mattie the truth.

Two hours later, Mary was declared fit to go home. The knife wound wasn't deep, but it had bled a lot. It was what had caused her to pass out. They'd treated the blood loss, put her on antibiotics, and sent her home. Caleb told her mom he would drive her and stay until she and Mattie got there.

Mary dragged herself up the steps and unlocked the door. Before going in, she glanced over at the Flynns'. She could see Caleb's dad's car still sitting in the driveway along with two others she didn't recognize.

"Why don't we sit outside for a while?" Caleb suggested when she couldn't bring herself to open the door. Memories of what had just happened were still too fresh for her to be comfortable going inside.

She gave him a grateful smile and sat next to him on the porch swing. Caleb was sweet when he wasn't showing his arrogant gene.

"Are you okay?" he asked, turning to look at her. "It had to bring back some really horrifying memories for you."

She looked over at the Flynns', the last few

hours engraved in her head. It had brought back every moment of her captivity, every awful thing Mrs. Olsen had done to her. She shivered thinking about it.

"It did." She looked down, her fingers kneading at each other. "I survived it, though."

"Yeah, you did." Caleb's voice held a grin. "You're a fighter."

Another shiver snaked down her spine. Caleb's words mirrored Deleriel's. He'd promised it wasn't the last time they'd see each other. It made Mary's chest tighten with anxiety.

"Hey." Caleb's finger lifted her chin, much as it had that day in the woods by the lake. "You're doing it again. Don't look away when someone compliments you."

Well, dang. Mary was beginning to understand Mattie's aggravation with Dan's eyes. He and Caleb had the same eyes, and they were drowning her right now in warmth and fuzzy feelings.

"About the party tomorrow night..." Caleb leaned in.

"Yes?" she asked breathlessly.

"I made up my mind," he whispered, coming closer.

"You did?"

"Mmmhmm." His breath tickled her lips. "It *is* a date."

Then he kissed her.

Mary relaxed against him and let all the warm, fuzzy feelings replace the fear and the panic she'd felt all night.

Maybe things were finally looking up for her.

***

Deleriel watched the girl from the shadows. She was the most curious creature he'd seen since he'd fallen.

His eyes flickered from the demon hunter she was kissing to the ones now at the boy's house.

Tricky, but Deleriel always got what he wanted, and he wanted the ray of sunshine that was Mary Cross.

The End of Book 3.5

Acknowledgements

First, I have to say thank you to all *The Ghost Files* fans. I took a year off from writing and you guys kept harassing me almost daily for more *Ghost Files*. You kept the series alive and made me remember why I love my crazy world of spooks. This series would not be where it is today without each and every one of you. The unfaltering faith in this series brings me to tears.

I also need to say thank you to all the folks over at Wattpad, from the readers to the staff at corporate. My Watty readers are amazing. You guys are the main reason *The Ghost Files* survived. I had over fifty agents tell me the book wasn't good enough to sell in the YA market. You all proved them wrong. Your support is the reason I have a publishing deal for the series and a movie deal as well. Thank you. Wattpad HQ…what can I say? You guys rock, from Caitlin to Gavin. You have helped me so much, and I will always support and promote Wattpad because of how great you guys are.

I have to thank Limitless Publishing. I have had a really bad two years, part of why I took time off. They never pressured me about any of my books with them. Instead, they supported me and gave me the time and space I needed to deal with some really hard blows. Jennifer, Jessica, Lori, Dixie…just a *BIG* thank you. Without the support of y'all, I'd still be struggling to find a home for my personal brand of crazy ☺

Huge shout out to my girls and fellow authors,

DelSheree Gladden, Angela Fristoe, and Susan Stec. Your unfailing support and advice keep me on the straight and narrow. I can still remember when we were all on The Next Big Writer, unpublished, dreaming big, and now we all are published and doing great! (FYI...check these girls out on Amazon...not so subtle hint, lol)

Thanks to Jennifer Hewitt for just being awesome every day and doing everything she can to help out and make my life easier so I can spend time writing instead of mired down in everything else.

My family deserves an award for just putting up with my mood swings while trying to get back in the groove of writing again...no make that sainthood. Yup, definitely sainthood. You guys believe in me even when I don't believe in myself and that's why I love you so much.

Love you all,

~Apryl Baker

About the Author

So who am I? Well, I'm the crazy girl with an imagination that never shuts up. I LOVE scary movies. My friends laugh at me when I scare myself watching them and tell me to stop watching them, but who doesn't love to get scared? I grew up in a small town nestled in the southern mountains of West Virginia where I spent days roaming around in the woods, climbing trees, and causing general mayhem. Nights I would stay up reading Nancy Drew by flashlight under the covers until my parents yelled at me to go to sleep.

Growing up in a small town, I learned a lot of values and morals, I also learned parents have spies everywhere and there's always someone to tell your mama you were seen kissing a particular boy on a particular day just a little too long. So when you get grounded, what is there left to do? Read! My Aunt Jo gave me my first real romance novel. It was a romance titled "Lord Margrave's Deception." I remember it fondly. But I also learned I had a deep and abiding love of mysteries and anything paranormal. As I grew up, I started to write just that and would entertain my friends with stories featuring them as main characters.

Now, I live in Huntersville, NC where I entertain my niece and nephew and watch the cats get teased by the birds and laugh myself silly when they swoop down and then dive back up just out of reach. The cats start yelling something fierce...lol.

I love books, I love writing books, and I love entertaining people with my silly stories.

Facebook:
https://www.facebook.com/authorAprylBaker

Twitter:
https://twitter.com/AprylBaker

Wattpad:
http://www.wattpad.com/user/AprylBaker7

Website:
http://www.aprylbaker.com/

Blog:
http://mycrazzycorner.blogspot.com/

TSU:
http://www.tsu.co/Apryl_Baker

Goodreads:
http://www.goodreads.com/author/show/5173683.A
pryl_Baker

Linkedin:
http://www.linkedin.com/pub/april-
baker/44/6b9/3a4

Authorgraph:
https://www.authorgraph.com/authors/AprylBaker

38024545R00061

Made in the USA
Middletown, DE
11 December 2016